ANTONIO TABUCCHI

# Stories with Pictures

Translated from the Italian by Elizabeth Harris

*archipelago books*

Archipelago Books
232 3rd Street #A111
Brooklyn, NY 11215
www.archipelagobooks.org

Distributed by Penguin Random House
www.penguinrandomhouse.com

Cover art: Giancarlo Savino, *Into the Dark of the Night* (detail), 1993

This book was made possible by the New York State Council on the Arts with the
support of Governor Andrew M. Cuomo and the New York State Legislature.

Funding for this book was provided by a grant from the Carl Lesnor
Family Foundation.

Archipelago Books also gratefully acknowledges the generous support of the
National Endowment for the Arts, Lannan Foundation, the Nimick Forbesway
Foundation, Lannan Foundation, and the New York City
Department of Cultural Affairs.

PRINTED IN CANADA

*For Elvira Sellerio*

# Contents

Author's Note. . . . . . . . . . . . . . . . . . . . . . . . . . . . . . 3

*Adagios*

So Long. . . . . . . . . . . . . . . . . . . . . . . . . . . . . . . . . 7

Flames. . . . . . . . . . . . . . . . . . . . . . . . . . . . . . . . . 17

Rainy Evening on a Holland Dike . . . . . . . . . . 23

Bernardo Soares on Holiday . . . . . . . . . . . . . . . 29

Faraway . . . . . . . . . . . . . . . . . . . . . . . . . . . . . . . 35

The Painter and His Creatures . . . . . . . . . . . . . 41

A Window onto the Unknown . . . . . . . . . . . . . 47

Story of the Man of Paper . . . . . . . . . . . . . . . . . 53

Dreaming with Dacosta . . . . . . . . . . . . . . . . . . . 63

On the Road to Möbius . . . . . . . . . . . . . . . . . . . 73

An Unforgettable Night. . . . . . . . . . . . . . . . . . . 81

Hold it – Don't Wake Up. . . . . . . . . . . . . . . . . . 87

A Discovered Letter . . . . . . . . . . . . . . . . . . . . . . 91

Double Enigma . . . . . . . . . . . . . . . . . . . . . . . . . 95

The Minotaur's Headaches . . . . . . . . . . . . . . . . 101

A Midwinter Night's Dream . . . . . . . . . . . . . . 105

*Andantes, con Brio*

The Heirs are Grateful . . . . . . . . . . . . . . . . . . . . 111

A Difficult Decision . . . . . . . . . . . . . . . . . . . . . 127

The Lady-with-the-Hat . . . . . . . . . . . . . . . . . . 131

A *Curandeiro* in the City on the Water . . . . . . . 139

*Ariettas*

The Arrival of Doctor Pereira . . . . . . . . . . . . . 151

The Fixed Traveler . . . . . . . . . . . . . . . . . . . . . . 155

Like a Mirror . . . . . . . . . . . . . . . . . . . . . . . . . . 159

Portraits of Stevenson . . . . . . . . . . . . . . . . . . . 163

Spices, Lace, Distant Journeys . . . . . . . . . . . . . 167

Dear Wall, I'm Writing You . . . . . . . . . . . . . . 173

Diary of Crete, With Hues of Sinopia . . . . . . . 179

Outside Terraces, Inside Terraces . . . . . . . . . . . 191

Parisian Cafés . . . . . . . . . . . . . . . . . . . . . . . . . . 195

For a Catalogue That Isn't . . . . . . . . . . . . . . . . 199

Translator's Note . . . . . . . . . . . . . . . . . . . . . . . 203

Art . . . . . . . . . . . . . . . . . . . . . . . . . . . . . . . . . . 204

# Stories with Pictures

# Author's Note

Painting has often moved my pen. If I hadn't gone to the Prado one distant afternoon in 1970 and then been "held captive" by Velázquez's *Las Meninas*, unable to tear myself away until closing, I would never have written "The Reversal Game." The same can be said of the frescoes of the San Marco convent, for these affected me deeply as a child and I often revisited them as an adult, until one fine day, they pushed their way onto the pages of *The Flying Creatures of Fra Angelico*. There are also passages from *Tristano Dies* that wouldn't exist without Goya's *Dog Buried in Sand*.

From image to voice, the way is brief if the senses respond. The retina communicates to the eardrum, "speaks" in the ear of the one looking; and for those of us who write, the written word is voiced – is first heard in our head. Sight, hearing, voice, word. But this current flows back and forth, departs again from where it arrived, returns again from where it departed. And the word, returning, carries with it other images that weren't there before: the word has invented them. Such is the case with many of these stories. If the image has sparked the writing, the writing in turn has led the image elsewhere, to that hypothetical elsewhere that the painter didn't paint. The story stirred by the visible has grabbed hold of What-we-see, so it can wander freely in the territory the artist kept hidden from us, what the artist could have painted or photographed, but didn't. "The soul imagines what it can't see," Leopardi tells us. The territory of writing is the imagination that goes beyond the image; it is the story of the pictures but also the turning over, the proliferation of these pictures, the story of the unknown that surrounds them.

I once promised Elvira Sellerio I'd put my "stories with pictures" together into one volume. In the meantime, with the passing years, other pictures, other images caught my eye and were translated into writing. While we write, we don't realize that writing and time are inversely proportional: the pages grow, and time dwindles. This book is only just coming out now. But promises don't expire.

Antonio Tabucchi
Lisbon, January 2011

*Adagios*

# So Long

And who would get postcards? Thinking about it, he wondered if he should make a list, because once you reach your destination, you always forget. He found a sheet of paper in the desk, sat down, and started coming up with names and addresses. He lit a cigarette. He'd write down a name, think it over, take a drag of his cigarette, and write down another. After he finished, he copied the names into his datebook and tore up the paper. He set the datebook on top of his shirts, in his open suitcase. He looked around, studying the room, like he was trying to remember what he might've forgotten – it was going to be a long trip. Then he remembered the postcards he'd bought in an art gallery and left on the bookshelf. He started sorting through them, to see if they might work for this upcoming trip. Not really, he told himself, they don't really work, what's a postcard of Le Marche got to do with South America? But then he also thought how nice the stamps would look; in Peru, for instance, he'd buy stamps with parrots, there had to be stamps with parrots in Peru, plus stamps with faces of pre-Columbian gods, smiling, inscrutable masks, masks of gold or glazed enamel – he'd seen an exhibit once at Palazzo Reale – there had to be stamps of those places, too. Actually, he liked the idea, because typical tourist postcards were so ugly, the colors always too bright, fake colors, and all the cards alike, whether they came from Mexico or Germany. So this was far more original: a postcard with "from Ascoli" written on it when it came from Oaxaca or Yucatán or Chapultepec (was that it?) – these names of places where he'd go.

Where he should have gone with Isabel, if she were still here. But she wasn't, she was gone before they could. For fifteen years, they thought about that trip, but it wasn't a trip you could take just like that, especially for two people in their profession. It took time, availability, money – all things that weren't there before. Now they were, but Isabel wasn't. He went to the desk, found a picture of Isabel and set it in his suitcase, beside the datebook and the postcards. It was a picture of them, arms linked, standing in Piazza San Marco in Venice, surrounded by pigeons, with vaguely stupid smiles on their faces, like people smile for a camera. Were we happy? he thought. And he recalled how Isabel took his hand on the boat taxi and whispered: "Well, if we can't get to South America right now, at least we're in Venice."

Odd when pictures lie flat: he and Isabel, surrounded by pigeons, with San Marco below, and them staring up at the ceiling. It bothered him, their eyes in that picture, staring up at the ceiling, so he turned the picture over and said: "I'm taking you along, Isabel, you're going on this trip, too, we'll travel all over the place, Mexico, Colombia, Peru, and we'll have a great time and write postcards, and I'll sign them for us both; I'll sign your name, too, it'll be just like you're with me – no – you *will* be with me, because as you well know, I always take you along."

He quickly added up the things left to do; the last things, he thought, feeling like someone who wouldn't be coming back. And all at once, he understood that he wouldn't be coming back, that he'd never set foot inside this apartment again, this apartment where he'd spent almost his entire life longing to be in exotic places with mysterious names like Yucatán and Oaxaca. He shut off the gas valve, the water valve, switched off the circuit breaker, closed the shutters. Standing by the windows, he realized how hot it was. Of course – it was August fifteenth. And he thought that he'd chosen a perfect day to leave, a day when everyone was on vacation, crowded onto the beaches, everyone far away, gone from the cities, packed together like ants invading a little rampart of sand.

It was nearly one, but he wasn't hungry. Even if he'd been up since seven and only had coffee. His train was at two thirty – plenty of time. He picked out a card with "Robinson Island" on the front, and on the back he wrote: *We're on Timultopec, a small island where Robinson could easily have been shipwrecked, never been happier, yours, Taddeo and Isabel.* He signed "Taddeo." No one called him Taddeo, his baptism name, but it just came to him. And then he wondered who he'd send the card to. But there was time for that. And then he chose another, one with some towers, and on the back he wrote: *This is the Machu Picchu mountain range, the air's incredible here, so long, Taddeo and Isabel.* Then he found another, one that was entirely blue, and on the back he wrote: *This is the blue we're living, a blue ocean, a blue sky, a blue life.* Then he found one with a church, maybe Santa Maria Novella, and on the back he wrote: *The South American baroque, a copy of Europe's, but vaguer, more visionary, love, Taddeo and Isabel.*

He wondered if he should bother trying to get a taxi, or if he should just take the bus. The station was only three stops away, and considering what day it was, he might be on the phone a good twenty minutes trying to call for a taxi; this really wasn't the day for a taxi, there weren't any – there wasn't even a car – the city was completely deserted. He spread a handkerchief over the picture and the postcards and carefully closed the suitcase. He looked around another time. He drew the blinds, patted his back pocket to check for his wallet, and headed down the hall to the entranceway. At the door he set his suitcase on the floor a moment and said out loud: "See you later, home. No – goodbye."

In the shade of the bus shelter, it wasn't so bad, though the street was dissolving into shiny puddles. At least there was a slight breeze, some relief. When he got off at the train station, he thought he might faint. But only for a moment – he felt dizzy for a moment – it was the blazing heat, of course, radiating off the stones, and the dazzling light, a light without shadow, the sun at its peak. The station clock read two. The lobby was deserted. Only one ticket counter was open, he got his ticket and looked around for a newspaper kiosk, but the kiosk was closed. His suitcase certainly wasn't very heavy. For such a long trip, he'd only brought along the bare essentials, the rest he'd buy a little at a time in the countries he'd visit when the opportunity or need arose. He glanced into the first-class waiting room, also deserted, he paused, considering, but the air was suffocating. Maybe the underpass is cooler, he told himself, or maybe there's at least a breeze under the platform roof. He walked slowly through the underpass, congratulating himself that his suitcase was so light, and he climbed the stairs to track three. It was completely deserted. No, the entire station was deserted, not one passenger. He noticed a small boy in a white shirt sitting on a bench, a carrying case of ice cream slung over his shoulder. The boy saw him, too, and rose, wearily shifted his case, and started toward him. When he was closer, he said: "You want an ice cream, mister?" He told him no thanks; and the boy took off his white cap and wiped his forehead.

"I shouldn't have bothered coming today," the boy said.

"You haven't sold much?"

"Three cones and a *cassata*. To passengers taking the one o'clock. But there won't be any more after yours – there's a strike on for three hours, except for intercity trains." He laid the case on the ground and pulled a stack of cards from his pocket. He arranged the cards on the edge of the bench seat, then tapped them with the back of his finger so they dropped to the ground. Those that fell he gathered and set aside. "These ones win," he explained.

"How old are you?" the man asked.

"Almost twelve," the boy answered, "this is the second summer I've sold ice cream at the station, my father has a kiosk at Piazza Santa Caterina."

"And your father's kiosk isn't enough?"

"Well, no. There's three of us kids. And life's pretty expensive these days, you know." Then, changing the subject, he said: "Are you going to Rome, mister?"

The man nodded but didn't answer. Then he said: "I'm going to Fiumicino. The Fiumicino Airport."

The boy slipped a card delicately between his index finger and thumb, like a paper airplane, and made his lips vibrate like an engine.

"What's your name?" the man asked.

"Taddeo. How about you?"

"Taddeo."

"Weird," the boy said, "we have the same name. Not too many Taddeos out there – it's not a very common name."

"And what do you plan to do later?"

"What do you mean later?"

"When you grow up."

The boy thought a moment. His eyes were very bright, and you could see his imagination churning. "I'm going on a bunch of trips," he said. "I'll travel all over the world and have all different jobs, here, there, everywhere I go."

The station bell began to sound and the boy gathered up his cards. "That's the intercity," he said, "I have to get ready to sell my ice cream."

He'd hardly finished before the announcement came over the loudspeaker. "Have a good trip," the boy said as he walked away, shifting his case on his shoulder. He moved toward the head of the track, clearly to walk along the platform in the opposite direction of the arriving train, for the possibility of more sales. Just then, the train emerged from the thick curtain of heat that veiled the outlying buildings. The man stood up, suitcase in hand.

It was a very long train, the cars were the more modern kind, with corridor windows that didn't lower, so those passengers wanting ice cream stood at the doors. The man watched with pleasure: the boy was making a killing. The two conductors who'd stepped onto the platform took a good look down the track, then one whistled, and the doors slid shut. And the train started off. The man watched it dissolve into waves of heat, he went back to his bench and opened his suitcase. The boy came over, tucking his change into the coin purse around his waist.

"You didn't leave?"

"Apparently not."

"What about Fiumicino?" the boy asked, "you'll miss your flight."

"Oh, there'll be others," the man answered, smiling. He took the postcards out of his suitcase and showed them to the boy. "These are my cards," he said, "want to see?"

The boy took them and started studying them, one by one. "I like this one of Elba Island," he said, "I've been there, too. And this one of Venice, with all the little birds."

"They're pigeons," the man said, "Venice is full of pigeons, all kinds, all colors, like the parrots in Peru."

"Really?" the boy asked, doubtful, "you're not bullshitting me, are you?"

"No, no. It's true. And look at this one that's completely yellow. This one's of Ascoli, a city that's completely yellow, with flecks of gold, it's all the light effects."

"Pretty," the boy said, convinced now. And then he asked: "How many?"

"Thirty."

"So," the boy said, getting down to business, "you want to trade?"

The man seemed lost in thought.

"Trade me for my cards," the boy said, "like for this one with the parrots, I'll give you a Maciste and two Ferrari Formula 1s. Plus I have ten singers." The man seemed to be thinking, then he said: "You know what – just keep them. I don't need them anymore." He set the cards on the boy's ice-cream case, picked up his suitcase, and headed for the underpass.

As he started down the stairs, the boy called after him. "Hey, that doesn't seem right – but thanks," he shouted. "Really, thanks!"

The man waved. "So long," he said to himself.

# Flames

Toward evening, a disciple came and told me to go to the Master's house, so I put on my light cloak and stepped into the night; I walked through the city of Agrigento, down the paths leading out to the countryside. The moon was full and red, blood-red, and was surrounded by a yellow halo, as though on fire, and the countryside was nearly bright as day and rose-colored, like flesh. There were two lit torches on the door to his house; I went inside and heard whispering in the front hall, the servants came forward, and they bowed and took me to the Master's room. It was profoundly quiet, the only sounds the crickets outside and the warm breathing of the summer night.

The disciples were gathered around the Master's bed. In the dim light, I recognized a few friends, and we nodded to each other. They told me that Empedocles had been asleep a short while, that he'd been extremely agitated before, strangely agitated: his fingers had fluttered, his only movement. And while they fluttered like strands of spider web vibrating in the breeze, his body lifted slightly off the bed, and there it stayed, suspended, floating, as if it might fly out the window, into the night. And then, very slowly, his body lowered to the sheets again and was still, so still, he didn't seem to be breathing, but he was breathing, you had to bring your ear near his mouth to feel it, a thread of air, a lonely thread from deep inside his body, like the modulated notes of a flute. And so I came closer to hear, but I didn't need to come closer, because Empedocles's corporeal flute had begun to play and into the room crept an odd melody, hard to describe, like a joyful song composed from tormented notes. Then the song ended and the room was again profoundly quiet. The maidservants came in carrying drinks, they seemed to be taking advantage of this interval: and it really was only an interval, my fellow disciples told me, because Empedocles had been like this since nightfall: levitating, singing, then lying inert, as though in a heavy torpor.

We drank and talked about the stars. And what our Master had taught us, the make-up of the universe, its lights and shadows, and how the celestial bodies move in their vast sidereal spaces, following a dance all their own that men didn't seem to understand. Then someone, one of the oldest disciples, recalled Empedocles's feats with air and water, the time the wind blew over the plain for days, stripping the fruit off the trees, and how Empedocles had donkey hides strung across poles and set up on the hills, and the wind changed direction; or the time the people of Selinunte were dying from the plague, from the sickly vapors off the river, and Empedocles ordered two streams diverted into that sickly river, and so he cured the river and the people. He'd faced the elements, Empedocles had, and he grew to understand them: most of all, he understood fire, which is the beginning and the end, life and death, because it's from fire that we're born and to fire that we'll return, as we burn in the flames that control the ring of the universe. Then the elderly disciple was silent, and we all sat down on the floor, around the Master's bed.

The night wore on, and we gazed out the window, to the sky, quiet, absorbed in our thoughts of that great book where fire reigns, presiding over life, as the Master taught us. Until, finally, the moon appeared in the window. It was red, on fire, inflamed by summer, and hung low over the horizon, as if it longed to reach the land beyond the mountains. A square of moonlight played over the bed where our Master lay, and then something astonishing occurred.

His body began to quiver, as if a wind was blowing over him, his skin was no longer opaque, it grew brighter, then was transparent; and we could see the workings of his body, all the organs, the veins, viscera, and bones supporting the flesh. Empedocles's lips parted slightly, and we heard that song again, but it wasn't a song or a lament: it was a distant voice, piercing, almost a whistle, but with a modulated melody, too, with certain notes, like a harp's song, magical, indescribable. And when the notes were at their most piercing, the Master's body lit on fire. It burned from within, as if he'd been smoldering on the inside: and we saw his veins redden, then glow white-hot in the spreading flames; then the fire spread outside his body, thin tongues of flame flickering over him, and we watched with wonder, powerless to speak. Then his body rose and floated in midair, and a small flame escaped his mouth, others darted from his ears, his nostrils; the fiery lava in his veins overflowed, spilling into his muscles and flesh. The torches had gone out, but the room was filled with light as Empedocles slowly burned like an enormous, silent torch, his body disintegrating into moths of ash that fluttered out the window.

We stayed through the night, until his body was consumed. And after he joined the fire of the universe, where all things originate and all things must return, we closed the shutters and said those words we always recited with the Master before the stars. The blood-red moon dipped below the hills, carrying our Master away, carrying him off to join the stars in space, the fiery bodies spinning in the grips of a precise, unchanging dance that men can never understand.

# Rainy Evening
# on a Holland Dike

It's like we're in a Simenon novel, the man said, the rainy night, the small-town folks we've come across, the Holland dike, this pipe of mine. By the way – sorry – do you mind if I smoke? He turned off the ignition and flipped on the parking lights.

She looked at him, and he smiled. When did you start smoking a pipe? she asked.

After my heart attack, the man said, twenty years ago, you don't inhale with a pipe, but the smell makes it look like you do.

So, now for the million-franc question, she said, what was your favorite painting?

Well, he said, I have to admit I had problems with the entire show, I'm not crazy about these mega-shows, I find them disorienting, it's like stuffing your face – stuffing your face on caviar – but it's still stuffing your face.

So why'd you go? she asked.

Simple, he said, so I wouldn't miss an appointment.

You thought we'd run into each other? she asked, surprised.

He smiled again. Of course not, he said, imagine that, with all those people, after all this time. It was just a platonic appointment, an homage to times gone by, an allegiance to a painter we both loved. Remember Arles?

That was in '58, she said.

No, he said, sure of himself, it was '59.

No, she said sweetly, it was '58. In '59 we went to Saint-Rémy, to visit the Saint-Paul-de-Mausole mental hospital, and then we went to Auvers-sur-Oise, where he died. We were in Arles in '58 – it was September.

He scratched his head, then loosened his tie. I remember the opposite, he said, but you're right as usual.

Because I kept a diary, she said, that's all. But, you still haven't answered my question: what was your favorite painting?

I should have kept a diary, too, he said, skirting her question, I've left that entire period to memory instead, and we all know that memories are full of holes, composed of scraps.

But don't you think diaries are full of holes, too? she said. I've tried rereading mine, to recapture those days, and it's full of holes, they're just fragments, and it feels like it's written by a different person, I mean, by the same person who's also a different person.

I have my photos, he said. And then he went on: wait, while we're on the subject, I have the perfect song, an old Charles Trenet tune. He turned on the tape deck and inserted the tape. Then he relit his pipe and cracked the window. The rain was pouring down now. Water in every direction, he said, water from the sky, water to the right, water to the left, we're surrounded by water. *Une photo, vielle photo de ma jeunesse*, he sang along softly with Trenet.

Your photos have been all over the world, she said, I know they had a huge tribute to you in New York, you're the most famous photographer out there right now.

Let's just say I was, he answered, now it's time to make way for the young.

So, do you have the photos from back then?

I've got every last one of them, every last one of them from our Provence. I could make prints and send them to you.

I don't know, she said, maybe not, I might prefer seeing them in my memory. But I'd like to have one of you, of your face from back then.

There's that self-portrait I did in the mirror at a hotel in Arles, he murmured, do you remember? What hotel was that?

I can't remember, but it was on Rue Lépic, I'm sure it was on Rue Lépic.

How on earth do you remember the street?

Because, she said, it's the same street where he lived and painted, he had an atelier on the corner of Rue Lépic, and we stayed in a small hotel on that same street because it seemed like a good omen.

Was it a good omen?

She pretended not to understand.

Was it a good omen? he repeated, louder.

Of course it was, she said, it was something great, but then the clock hands swallow everything in an instant, it's awful, don't you think?

What's awful? he said.

This, she said. You go through life and practically don't notice, and then you only think about it later, when life's gone by.

He was quiet, then he said: I can't decide between *L'eglise d'Auvers-sur-Oise* and *La chamber de Vincent à Arles*, the 1888 version, maybe that one.

Ah, she said after a moment, you finally got around to answering my question.

And what about you? he asked, what was your favorite?

*La sieste*, she said, do you remember it, two peasants, a man and a woman, lying on some sheaves of wheat. It's midday, everything's calm, the distant sky, a rich blue, they're surrounded by the golden-yellow wheat, you can practically hear the cicadas.

So why that one? he asked.

Well, she said, for sentimental reasons, because we took a siesta ourselves once, I'm not sure you remember, it was near the Langlois Bridge, no, where the Langlois Bridge once was, anyway it was around there, we drove by and decided we'd have a picnic, I bought some bread and cheese, and then we fell asleep in a pile of straw.

I thought it would be the *Tournesols*, he said.

What? she said.

No, he said, I mean, I was sure you'd pick the *Tournesols*.

The rain was falling even harder. With the wind now, eddics of water swirled in the lighthouse beams.

You know what this rain makes me think about, she said, it makes me think about time.

How so? he asked.

I'm not sure, she said.

Speaking of, he said, what time do you have?

She looked at her watch. Almost midnight, she said.

Maybe we should be getting back, he said, I need to be in bed soon, doctor's orders. He turned on the ignition, and started backing up the car. The sea was calm, quiet, as if appeased by the rain.

I've never been on a dike in Holland, she said. It's a strange feeling.

Where do you live now? he asked.

Paris, she said. How about you?

Geneva, he answered, for tax purposes.

Do you remember *L'Anguille*? she asked.

Sure, he said, a restaurant, right, but not in Arles, where was it? – and how was it – remind me again.

It was close to Sète, she said, the owner used to be a chef on an ocean liner, his wife was an alcoholic, no one ever went, but the food was incredible, we discovered it by accident, you were crazy about the *grenouilles à la provençale*.

Should we have lunch tomorrow? he asked.

I leave in the morning, she said, I only came for the show.

So many things, he said.

So many things what? she said.

So many things all told, he said.

She sneezed and asked him to turn on the heat.

# Bernardo Soares on Holiday

On December 24, 1934, Bernardo Soares woke up early and started putting on his best clothes. He slipped on the jacket his boss had given him as a gift, a beautiful, heavy tweed jacket that the Vasques firm imported from London, and he pulled on his shoes and a pair of spotless spats. He carefully packed the small suitcase sitting open on the bureau. He laid some underwear inside, then various changes of shirts, the gray pullover, his nasal drops, cough salve, and laudanum solution for insomnia, a paraffin lamp, the Uzbekistan travel guide for the trip he'd always dreamed of taking to Samarkand, and the last notebook of his diary, already half-filled. It was Christmas Eve and for some reason, he thought this might be his last Christmas. And truthfully, this didn't bother him much; his one regret in life was that he'd never been to see the golden domes of Samarkand.

Mr. Vasques had promised to send along his car and driver at nine sharp, and though it was only eight thirty, Bernardo Soares stepped over to the window. He thought he might pass the time by doing something useful, so he started to write a Christmas letter to his only friend. Perhaps *friend* wasn't exactly the right word, he was more of an acquaintance, really, but they were friendly toward one another, dining together almost nightly on the first floor of an old restaurant in Baixa and talking about literature. Bernardo Soares took up his pen and paper and standing, leaning against the dresser, he wrote:

Dear Mr. Fernando,

This Christmas, we won't be able to share a meal at our usual restaurant. I'm going to spend the holidays, at least until New Year's, in Cascais, in a house owned by an Italian-Portuguese export-import firm, Modica & Guimarães Limited, which has an excellent relationship with the firm that I work for. Mr. Vasques, my employer, keeps the keys to this house for the owners, as they live in Paris and only go to Cascais a few weeks over the summer. I believe this house will be slightly inconvenient, as there's no heat and it's been unoccupied for some months now. Not to mention the floors are in bad shape and there's no electricity. But I believe I'll be able to remedy this situation by wearing heavy clothes and bringing along a paraffin lamp. As I told you the last time we saw each other, I wish to describe a dawn and a sunset over the sea: I'd like to observe for myself the light variations one can find at these particular times of day. Apparently, the house where I'm going to spend my holidays has a nice terrace overlooking the sea, so if I spend a few hours out there, I shouldn't find it difficult to develop a palette of words to describe the light at dawn and at sunset. But why am I writing, my dear Mr. Fernando, and for whom? Quite frankly, I'm not sure I can answer this. I'm writing for myself, of course, because I am my sole reader, and I have no desire, have never considered publishing what I write. And so I write to tell myself, as if I were someone else, the things that I myself think in this solitary life of mine; and also to appease the disquiet that accompanies my nights. A very merry Christmas to you, and my best wishes for a happy 1935.

Sincerely yours,

Bernardo Soares

Just then a horn sounded, and he knew Mr. Vasques's car had arrived. He slipped the letter into his pocket, promising himself once again that he'd mail it on the way; he snapped shut his suitcase and left down the stairs. Mr. Vasques's chauffeur stood waiting, leaning against the car and smoking a cigarette. Bernardo Soares said hello and set his suitcase in the trunk. Please stop at the coal vendor's on the corner, he said, I have something to pick up.

The coal vendor was waiting by the door, already holding Sebastião on his perch. Sebastião was an old parrot who could say a few words, and the coal vendor had promised to loan him to Bernardo Soares over the holidays, so he wouldn't feel too lonely in Cascais. He set Sebastião on the back seat, and they were off. It was a beautiful sunny day, and not too cold out: it didn't feel like Christmas Eve in the least. The chauffeur, who knew all of Severa's *fados* by heart, asked if it would be all right if he sang one to himself, and Bernardo Soares, though he didn't much care for *fado*, told him to go right ahead. When they reached Cruz Quebrada, the road was backed up a bit because a horse had collapsed in front of its heavy cart and now lay across the roadway. The cart-driver, hurling

· 31 ·

curses, was trying to get the animal to its feet, but clearly, the poor beast had no intention of rising: its head rested on the pavement, the eye glassy and staring. Horse steak, the chauffeur said, that will be its Christmas. After Cruz Quebrada, the chauffeur finally stopped singing and Bernardo Soares could concentrate on the countryside and the variations of light on the horizon. As they drove through Paço d'Arcos, he asked the chauffeur to make a quick stop at the post office and he hurried out of the car to mail his letter. Sebastião was asleep on his perch and the ocean was a metallic blue.

Bernardo Soares had never been to Cascais, and as they drove through, he stared out the car window at that charming fishing village, at the villas on the edge of town, owned by rich Lisboners. The chauffer had turned onto Guincho Street, a deserted road winding along the ocean cliffs. They drove through the single iron gate that rose in the midst of a park, and the car stopped. We're here, the chauffer said. Bernardo Soares couldn't believe his eyes. He stared at the house: he counted twenty windows. It was a magnificent villa, though the façade was worn from salt and storms. He removed Sebastião and his suitcase from the car, the chauffeur opened the door to the house and gave him the keys. Happy holidays, Mr. Soares, the chauffeur said, and he drove away.

Bernardo Soares was left alone in that green space; he sat down on the steps and stared out to the sea. Once again, he thought that this would be his final Christmas, but also that it didn't matter. Then he took out a pack of Provisórios and started smoking a cigarette.

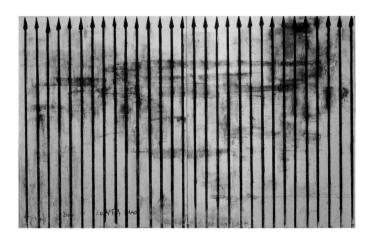

# Faraway

My darling,

And faraway, faraway in time, an expression on someone else's face might remind you a little of my face, of this I'm certain. My darling, I started painting behind the fence. Strange how iron bars can signal other times: it reminded me of an inmate once, back in that period when I used to teach painting at a penitentiary located on a small island, this man was serving a life sentence for murder (they were all in that prison for life), they were all murderers, I'm not sure what sort of murder it was, a crime of passion, no doubt, I think he killed someone who'd tried to sleep with his girl while he was working far away, way up North, in an automobile plant, and he'd left home with a cardboard suitcase. He must have been one of Rocco's brothers, you know what I mean, that's what he made me think of, and the sitting judge granted that he could have a drawing instructor, you probably think that's strange, and so the ministry offered me the job and I was only too eager to accept, because it wasn't exactly the best of jobs teaching drawing at various middle schools in a village in Maremma Tuscany, and this would be an adventure; Sundays, I took the small ferry that brought the inmates' relatives over, we'd reach the island by about nine in the morning, my "lesson" went from eleven to one, he'd skip lunch, poor guy, and then I was free to wander the island until seven at night, when the last ferry left. It was May of the year Idontrecall, I was practically a boy, and to play "the teacher" at the prison, I went around in a jacket and tie, because I thought this would give me more authority with the warden and the guards, but once I left, I'd run to the other side of the island, toward the cliff; there were sand dunes by the rocks, with wild myrtle shrubs and other herbs I didn't recognize, they were extremely fragrant, you can't imagine that smell, or maybe you can, because you know that island – or maybe you don't – I can't remember if you ever went, and I'd toss my jacket and shirt into the bushes and strip naked, the rocks were scalding hot, but they were flat, I had to be careful not to slip, and of course there were all those sea urchins to watch out for, there were so many sea urchins.

I'd taken to carrying a Swiss army knife, one of those small, bulging red things with a thousand different functions: two blades, a nail clipper, a file, tiny scissors, even a corkscrew. What a great thing, the Swiss army knife! I wonder who invented it. Whoever it was deserves a special medal for services rendered to humanity; with a Swiss army knife, you feel free. I bet it was invented by an anarchist, a "Farewell to Lugano" type, or one of those others, locally bred, with their anthem about tearing down the Alps to see the sea. What a glorious utopia – toppling the mountains! On the rocks, in the evening, the horizon was mine alone. Some nights I skipped the return ferry, I'd have some bread in my pocket, a little salami from the tavern by the prison run by this big fellow who was also a pork butcher in the winter, he'd slaughter his pigs and make sausages, and he'd sell them with his own D.O.C. quality control label, a homemade stamp that was glued on, a white, red, and green star inside a tiny circle with the letters: WAFABM. What's that mean? I asked him one day, somewhat timidly. We All Finish As Butcher's Meat, he answered, that's what it means, that's what makes us all equal citizens.

I'd buy a bottle of red wine to go with my bread and salami, and this was also made on the island though not by the tavern keeper, it was his brother-in-law's wine, a bottle with no label but with a tarred cork, so the corkscrew on my Swiss army knife came in handy. What a strange wine, I'll never forget it, almost sweet but not sweet, if you ask me, it came from those "American" grapes, the kind used for grape jelly, and it tasted like juice, almost like there was no alcohol, but a couple of swigs and you'd start to feel drunk, light-headed and happy, like you'd reached a state forbidden by the laws of nature. That's how I feel right now, looking at you through this fence: no, in terms of seeing you, I don't actually see you, though I "know" you're there, that one of those shadows is yours.

But where was I – sorry. I was telling you about the inmate I once taught, so to speak, about the use of colors. Though he knew how to handle colors better than I did, you can't even imagine his seascapes in pastel, always the same subject, the same image, or so it seemed, a bit like Morandi, with his bottles that are always the same, only they change positions, are different colors, a bottle on the left was green, and he shifted it around and made it blue, and he was right, and so I asked him, this novice painter: but in this pink picture, what's this black dot to the left, on the horizon, and then in this yellow one, here it is again at the top, and in this other sky-blue one, it's there on the right, just on the horizon line, and in this other one that's cobalt blue, you can just make it out at the bottom, like it wants to escape. He looked at me like I deserved pity. That's time, he answered. That black dot is time? I asked. He looked at me again with pity in his eyes. Time, he said, is only a black dot. Haven't you figured that out yet, sir?

And so I sat down behind time, and I watch you from here. And I told myself that the best way to capture you was to paint the time you're in. A true painting is necessary, my darling: in a photo, that place is no longer there, the digital photo will print the time and date in the lower right-hand corner, but this is an obvious convention that has nothing to do with what's outside, only with what's inside the belly of that photographic device.

When someone seems close but is far away instead, it's called an optical illusion. But that's definitely not our situation, because for us, there's a ridiculous temporal illusion passing itself off as an optical illusion. But come now – a painter like me won't just let himself be tricked by some silly optical illusion, as if I didn't know it's all a matter of perspective. Listen, my darling, on this side of the iron bars, it's 2001. I'm well aware that you're in '89. You've been sitting there, on that bench in that beautiful garden since '89, and you haven't moved. Please don't lose yourself in someone else's eyes, because sometimes, faraway faraway in time, something in someone else's eyes, might remind you a little of my eyes, but please don't let yourself be distracted from your present, it's just a matter of the little misunderstandings that foolish time will try to slip past us if we pay it any mind. My arm's already through the rails, do you see? I'm waving to you, it's me, or else you come to this time of mine, squeeze past the bars, or I'll return to '89 and we'll repeat all the things we did together between '75 and '89, and why not? Repetition helps us understand things better – and do you think it would take much for me to efface, to erase, this fence I've almost finished, so it becomes a finished fence in name and deed? Go on – your move or mine?

# The Painter
# and His Creatures

The Painter is alone, completely alone, in his shabby apartment. He doesn't even own a cat, because he wants to be alone. It's night, and the city is asleep. Through the window, the streetlamps are veiled in rain. The Painter has prepared for a meeting with his creatures. On the table are glasses and bottles of wine. He has no idea which creatures will come tonight, who will respond to his summons. The Painter lays out sheets of paper like napkins. Then he arranges his watercolors on the table and dilutes them with water in several small bowls that he sets beside the paper, like magic food.

Mostly he's mixed blues, pale greens, and antique rose. He's prepared a number of blues: night blue, electric blue, sky blue, deep blue. Then he mixes up a milky pink, with a touch of blue. He favors blue, because he knows the creatures that will come are night creatures, from interstellar space. The Painter turns on a lamp, sips a glass of wine, toasts his soon-to-arrive visitors. And meanwhile the night is growing darker and now and then footsteps are heard outside, as someone goes by on the street. And yet this is a Mediterranean night, filled with rain and a sirocco wind. And we're in a Mediterranean city, though the Painter often stays in Northern Europe: snow-covered plains and small wooden houses, frozen rivers and seawalls. And he's brought back vivid impressions from these places, paintings seen in perfect, white museums, where people tiptoe and the light through the windows is milky white. From these places, he has carried an expressionism back with him, ghostly figures watered down by Mediterranean ways, until they resemble lemurs, gentle ghosts, unsettling, laughing figures, with smiles verging on mysterious sneers. So the Painter, he raises his glass and says: come, my visiting creatures. Then he takes his pencil and brushes and sits down in front of a sheet of white paper.

And here comes the first creature. It's crammed into a sort of transparent ovum, like a fetus from another planet. It's from a distant galaxy and has taken light years to get here, to this warm Mediterranean city where lights shimmer like the moon on a curving gulf. This character is warm, pale, with extremely dark, inquisitive eyes that study the Painter and the empty dining room. The creature is surrounded by the nocturnal blue of its cosmic space, where matter halts and opens to black holes. It doesn't know how to speak our language, but for some reason, the Painter knows the creature's language, and so they can talk. I was once a man like you, the Creature says, I lived in this city, in this apartment, but that was many years ago, so many, that you can't remember. And then

I left, like men do, I vanished from these walls and from this life, and found other places, far-off secret places, and for a long while I lived in a glacier of feelings and felt nothing, experienced nothing, until you woke me again and brought me here.

The Painter smiles and dissolves the Creature's face in two drops of wine. Here's to your transparency, he toasts. Then he lays the sheet of paper on top of a napkin and dips a brush into the pink.

It's an antique dirty rose, with a hint of brick-red: the creature that was forced to come has just shed its skin, is changing shape. A larva turning to a butterfly, its limbs extremely long and spindly: the creature already has the feet of a butterfly, with a torso that's still that of a man, or a woman, it's hard to tell. Maybe a woman-man. Both at once, because this is a being in transformation, and the prearranged signs are visible, feminine and masculine, imprinted in its genetic makeup. This is a woman, a beautiful woman with beautiful characteristics who's becoming a man. Which is very difficult: the opposite is ordinary, almost boring. The Painter makes the creature comfortable and raises his glass in a toast. Then he moves to the bowls of blue. And with the blue, clowns come. And they don't just look like clowns, they act like clowns. And they too come from far away. Very far away. They leap, somersault, curl up into balls, writhe like grubs. And at the same time, they study the world. The world that is this room. And the Painter says: don't worry, we'll spend the night together and together we'll watch the sun rise over the gulf.

He arranges these clownish creatures on the napkins and toasts once more. His head's spinning a little by now, but he's not drunk, just happy. And in the distance, a church bell rings, five times. It's dawn. The Painter throws the windows open and looks over the gulf. It's magnificent, a blue haze spreading and lights going out in the rising glow.

Goodbye, my creatures! the Painter says. And he gathers up his watercolors. The beings are all lined up in a row on the napkins. And they gaze at him with the absent gaze of creatures accustomed to the night and unfamiliar with the day. I'm shutting you up in the pages of a book, the Painter tells them, so you'll be more comfortable. He closes the windows, turns off the lamp, and heads off to bed. He'll sleep well, a dreamless sleep. He's dreamt enough already.

# A Window onto the Unknown

Why had he moved there? He didn't know. Actually, he did know. It was the landscape, because with the landscape, he could leave behind his disquiet: the enormous spaces, the fields, the silence, the houses from the past, when houses were homes, and inside, along with the people, there were tools and equipment, everything necessary for the everyday life that was happening all around, near these homes where they lived.

But one day an architect had come, a friend of his, a distinguished architect in the big cities where big buildings went up in glass and steel, beautiful to see, and the architect had told him: "This wall keeps out the landscape, you have to put in a window, it'll be like a painting inside your home, but a natural painting, with nature inside the frame, because you have to let nature in through the window, you can't banish it with a wall." And he used his arms to create an imaginary window on that kitchen wall, framing the shelves with their salt and pepper and oil and the pans hanging on a nail, and he went on: "Get rid of all this junk, stick it in the bread box or cupboard: I'll make you a travertine shelf for under the window, and you'll set a bowl on it, and a couple of apples or oranges, like a small, country altar, a humble still life to go with the majestic humility of the landscape." And he'd managed to reply: "No, please, not travertine, I don't want any travertine in this house."

"All right," the architect answered, "I'll do it in plaster and paint it to look like fake travertine, so you'll be able to tell it's just a simple, country-style plaster shelf trying to pass itself off as travertine. And no shutters or blinds, it faces north, so even though the sun's ferocious here, it won't really hit the table all that much, and you'll be able to see the twilight, because during the summer here, when night falls and the intense heat lifts, the sky turns cobalt blue, the treetops light up, turn an unusual green color, have you noticed the strange green cast of the trees? Green's a compound color, made up of yellow and blue, the leaves lose their blue and what's left is a yellow punctured by the dark of the first night shadows, like maps of unknown lands. The ideal thing would be just to leave it, to leave the window open to the air and wind, so the indoors simply flows into the outdoors and welcomes it in. And you, there, drinking your glass of wine, fixing your supper and listening to music – because I know you listen to music while you fix your supper – you wouldn't be facing a wall anymore, you'd be standing before an opening to everything around you. This would be ideal, but an architect has to put limits on what he really wants, because even here, there's winter, and the rain and wind would come in, so to avoid that, I'll install a sheet of Plexiglas, not even two centimeters thick, these days you barely notice

Plexiglas, it's practically like air, trust me, you'll almost want to stick your hand right through sometimes, to feel the night breeze. By the way, what do you like to listen to, while you're drinking your glass of wine and making your spaghetti, before you face the night and your thoughts that you'll transform to words on paper?"

"It depends," he'd answered, "Mozart, usually, but Chet Baker, too, especially when he sings in that low, gravelly voice, it eases my disquiet, it's like a lullaby, it settles me down, also because he'll drag the words out so much that I can't understand them, like an ancient dirge, and then he'll start playing his muted trumpet and carry you off."

Night was falling, the sky had gone cobalt blue, the trees were tinged with yellow, as though the green of the leaves had dropped away. He was fixing himself a plate of spaghetti with some honey mushrooms he'd plucked off a tree trunk, and he'd added a little honeysuckle and some local pecorino; he put on a Chet Baker record, looked up, and saw the house behind his own. Abandoned, the owner had told him, a family of farm workers used to live there, they'd come during the Polesine floods, whole family's been dead for years.

The windows on the second floor were lit up, a large window, and a smaller one that had to be the attic window. And on the façade, he saw an exact triangle of light that seemed to be projected, because there weren't any streetlamps in view. And low on the house, in the corner, there was a wheel against the wall that looked to be the rear wheel of a bicycle, but it was too large to be the rear wheel of a bicycle. And then he thought he saw a shadow slipping away behind that corner, into the dark, but he couldn't be sure, perhaps he'd imagined it. He walked over to the window, and on impulse, tried to put his hand through, like he was waving to someone who wasn't there or he was simply trying to reach to the outside. But his hand hit the Plexiglas. He laid his palm on it, then pulled back. The sweaty imprint remained a moment. He turned off the music and stood listening. He considered how strange it was to look at the reality surrounding him as if it were within reach and he thought: nothing's within reach, especially what you see, and sometimes, what's nearby is further than you think. He also considered phoning his architect friend, but maybe certain things couldn't be said over the phone – better to write these things down, otherwise they seemed foolish. A note was better. You opened a window onto the unknown for me, he'd write. But he'd write it tomorrow.

# Story of the Man of Paper

I

*What shall I, the astral emigrant, do in life?*

I've started off. You can see me. I'm dressed like a normal man. I'm carrying a normal briefcase. I'm disguised as a normal man. I walk along with the crowd. Left-right-left-right, forward, march, right leg forward, right arm going along with the right leg. Left-right-left, left leg following the right, left arm going along with the left leg. I enter the crowd. I'm looking for someone who will listen to me. Won't you listen? Hey, everybody, I'm talking to you – won't you listen? I'm the Witness – won't you listen?

## 2

*And the city, now, is like a map of my humiliations and failures*:

I'm the Witness. But let me ask you, what is a witness? – ectoplasm resembling air, in air the storm is born, the sound of a voice vanishes into air and air changes to a cloud, to fog, to nothing. I'd like a witness, myself. It's a windy day. My tie, like a flag, flutters in the wind. My tie is the flag of my country. My body is my country. The flag of my body waves in the wind of History. Ah, History, such a strange lady! She told me she's not responsible, that none of it's her fault, it all depends on her cousin, Clio, the one of memory. Come join us for tea, she told me, we have splendid cookies. Madame History's house is far away, but I'm used to walking. I walked all day. Such a windy day. My tie was waving in the wind. And what sort of wind could it be? In France the mistral blows, and sometimes the north wind. In Buenos Aires we get the sea breeze mostly. But this was the wind of History. Walking, walking, not finding Madame History's house. Did it not exist? I called Information. They sounded fairly alarmed. Why are you looking? they asked. I have to tell her about my neighbors, I explained. They were out on the terrace, enjoying the cool evening, when they heard someone knocking at the door. There were two gentlemen in uniform, and they asked: sir, do you see this, do you know what it is? Of course, my neighbor said, it's a gun. That is correct, good for you, said the two gentlemen who'd knocked on the door, it is indeed a gun, and a gun confers authority, so we are the authorities, and you'll come with us whether you like it or not, we really don't give a shit, because you, sir, are not a citizen, you're anonymous, you're the crowd, and you'll disappear into the crowd, like nothing, like a small cloud, into a sky full of clouds. And what will become of my body? my neighbor asked. Don't worry about your body, they answered, think about your soul, think about your country. But my soul is my body, my country is my body, my neighbor said. The two gentlemen started laughing hysterically. Did you hear that, they said, slapping each other on the back, that's a good one. This guy's a riot, and they shoved him into the car. His wife never saw him again. Her last memory of him was his voice calling as the car disappeared into the night: my body!

3

*Nothing's changed. Except perhaps the manners, ceremonies, dances. The gesture of the hands shielding the head has nonetheless remained the same.*

That's the story I wanted to tell Madame History, I explained to Information. And a neutral voice over the phone said: go on, then.

4

*The body writhes, jerks, and tugs, falls to the ground when shoved, pulls up its knees, bruises, swells, drools, and bleeds.*

Do you understand? Strange, but Information didn't seem to understand. As if a body was beyond comprehension. I was having a little trouble. How to explain a body? I said: a nose, do you have a nose? A head, do you have a head? Eyes, do you have eyes? And a mouth and arms and hands and feet and balls, all these things are a body, dear Information, do you understand? But the neutral voice over the phone only said: go into more detail.

5

*Nothing has changed. Except the run of rivers, the shapes of forests, shores, deserts, and glaciers. The little soul roams among these landscapes, disappears, returns, draws near, moves away, evasive and a stranger to itself, now sure, now uncertain of its own existence, whereas the body is and is and is and has nowhere to go.*

I was almost screaming now, and the even voice over the phone said: calm down, don't get too excited, tell us where you are, we'll come and help you. I left the receiver dangling in that phone booth and resumed walking. I met a lot of people, you know. One day, I found a woman. She lay stretched out on a couch, she was naked and I saw she had scars. She said: come, my friend, mate with me, misfortune will be the metronome of our intimacy. One day, I found a dog. Because even dogs exist and have a right to dogness, which is their nationality, their country. Then I found an elephant. It was a very hot day, the sun was ruthless. We set off walking toward a bright future, like Chaplin at the end of his movies. Please, the elephant told me, take me through a triumphal arch, I've already traced my circle and soon I'll want to step inside. We walked a long time because it wasn't possible to combine an arch with triumph, meaning, the arch was close but triumph was still a good ways off. Perhaps that's just how it goes, in life. We sat down on a park bench and were cooling our feet in the spray of a small fountain, when someone approached, disguised as a bishop but wearing a black leather Gestapo-style coat. He opened his coat to show the luger he kept below his armpit. Then he pulled out an identification card with the name: Friedrich Lefebvre. In Argentina, he said, I'd be Frederico, in France, Frédéric, but, he said, that's my code name, I'm a mercenary soldier, I work for the church of defamation, I turn gold to shit, I know everything about you both – especially you there – I know everything about everybody: put your hands up. That scum thought he knew everything, a degenerate, and at night in the barracks (we learned later) he took out a leather whip and sodomized himself with the handle. But he didn't know the language of elephants. What should I do, the elephant whispered, trunk to my ear. Whack him, I said, it's him or us, a matter of survival. The elephant whacked him. There's nothing better than the nice hard whack of an elephant trunk to free yourself from the scum working for the secret police.

6

*You work for the whirling, scattering wind; a terrible sentence, life.*

But I am a man of flesh. Heroes are made of iron. Men of iron crush men of flesh. In Argentina, they come at night. They cruise the neighborhoods in their Ford Falcons, no plates, headlights off. And men of flesh can find no shelter. Where's the Italian ambassador? He's not here, he's out to dinner. Where's the apostolic nuncio? He's not here, he's playing tennis with the general of the coup. Big-time fascists, the host on their tongue. And the man of flesh, crushed beneath the iron throng, becomes a man of paper. I am a man of paper. To escape the world, I've turned to paper, but I've locked the world inside this paper so I can tell its story.

### 7

*When left uncharmed, the snake will bite. But what does the charmer stand to gain?*

It's a matter of charming the charmer. I was searching for someone to charm the charmer. I found it, a hand, a human hand, the thumb, index finger, middle finger, to support a pencil or a brush. The human hand I found charms the charmer who charms the snake.

### 8

*Do you recognize me, air, you who knew things that once were mine?*

We were dropping from planes. Night flight. First, though, just a quick injection so you'll think you're in the clouds. We became a telephone directory of dropped numbers. Entirely of paper. The world's made of paper. The world ends up in a book, but someone already said that.

9

*No one can write a book. Since before a book can really be, it needs the dawn, the dusk, centuries, arms, and the binding and sundering sea.*

A hard wind blew, waves almost swallowing me, and I hoped those hands would catch me. Whose hands? I remembered the lesson of Princesse Bibesco, in the book on the West that the nuns had made me study. The only thing to do was be a *Bateau sur l'eau: la rivière, la rivière au bord de l'eau*. With these vain, childish words, my small paper boat set sail without a bottle, with no protective glass, sail on, sail on, toward what? Toward the unknown. The question had changed. It was no longer to be or not to be. The ocean didn't give a damn about that, and neither did the West. The question was: to be or to appear? To be or to disappear? I wasn't stylish, I was well aware, I didn't know how to slip on gloves from a Paris glove shop like Princesse Bibesco teaches. And I wasn't searching for gloved hands. I was searching for bare hands, for hands of flesh that would take me for a man of flesh and tell me: stay – this is your likeness.

10

*Exhausted from trying, we don't know where to go, strangers in our own city.*

But there still have to be hands, a single hand, a single eye, a single finger. Is there just one eye, one finger left on the face of the earth? We're in the billions after all, it's statistically possible. Hope is a matter of statistics.

Faith and Charity might be, too. Ah, art! Art that's useless yet also saves! Art that no one votes for, that has no place in parliament, you escape in the crowd, you enter the crowd, you are the crowd. We're all the crowd. Might there be two hands, a single finger that can shape an individual from a crowd? One individual, who represents the crowd? The entire crowd, what we are, we, humanity as a whole. But humanity reduced to just one individual is silly, says the flute-like voice of Information over the phone. All right, I'll admit it's silly. I'll be that for you, I'll be the clown. A clown of the third type. Not the happy clown, not the sad clown, according to the binary pattern we've binarily divided the world into. A normal clown. Does that surprise you? Did it never occur to you? Well, I'm a normal clown. I need hands so I can move, walk, navigate through space, time, and memories. For this is normalcy: space, time, memory.

11

*The only thing that doesn't exist is oblivion.*

And all the rest exists, all the rest can be portrayed. Life escapes, you pass through it and it escapes. Death escapes, it grabs hold of you and it escapes. Cities escape, you pass through them and they escape. And you, you escape as well, you can't tell your story because you escape. But the hand runs over the page, guides the nib or brush; life has escaped, but its image remains. The music's played, the notes have disappeared. But the score remains. Right here, in front of you. Do you all see it, how it's drawn in precise lines, legible, decipherable: waiting to be played.

Play it. Each one of you will play it on your own instrument. You have a cello you keep at your side like a beloved bride? You have a flute that's your classmate? You have a set of bagpipes you carry piggyback like a child? Play the score in your own way, play the music as you see fit. You have an ocarina? Take it from your pocket. You don't have any instrument at all? Try whistling. You don't know how? Try humming to yourselves, step onto the main square of this beautiful city carrying your vision of that score you saw, transform these images into a sound that's yours alone, play it with your music, coming home, even if you're tone-deaf – do it – *for the private gifts that I won't mention, for the music, that mysterious form of time. Day enters night. It doesn't go away.*

# Dreaming with Dacosta

The last time I saw António Dacosta was in a dream, in the Azores. He was creating his dream, and I came to visit. May I enter your dream, Maestro? I asked. He raised the canvas of the painting he was working on and answered: by all means, come into my painting, if you please.

I entered, and it was night. A real Azorian island night, blue and green. There was a moon at the center, above the landscape, and in that moon, a young man's face. I recognized *A flor, a máscara e eu adolescente*. The young man had his eyes closed, seemed to be sleeping, and beneath him was a blood lily. On the right, like a streetlamp in the night, an ancient mask watched me with wide, staring eyes. I wandered in that dream and felt strangely unsettled. Nostalgia, there was nostalgia in that dream, and an odd rapture, like an invisible fetish.

Dacosta, I said, I feel a sense of disquiet, your dream makes me uneasy, perhaps you could tell me why.

I feel uneasy, too, Dacosta answered.

Why? I asked.

Because the Portuguese Nun and the Knight of Two Lemons had to take a trip together, and then they wrote each other such terrible letters.

I don't understand, I said.

And I'm not sure what to tell you, Dacosta answered, the truth is, the Portuguese Nun and the Knight of Two Lemons, they wrote these letters back and forth, he flattered her, made promises the last night of his visit, they had a night of passion, a fine Portuguese passion, Camilo Castelo Branco's the one who could really describe it, then the Knight left at a gallop, galloped all the way across Spain, and wrote her a letter from Provence. Apparently, he was vacationing with some other woman.

Incredible, I said, and what about the Portuguese Nun?

Dacosta stepped forward. Sorry if I change dreams, he said, but I want you to see her, if only from a distance.

A few steps, and the landscape changed. Now we were by a window in a convent cell, and through the grillwork, you could see a nun. She was *La religieuse portugaise*. She wore a white veil and her eyes were lowered. Her face was smeared with clay, like an ancient mourning mask, and she was silently crying and staring at the letter from her lover. I couldn't bear to watch, it felt like a twisted nightmare, such grief in that face, such yearning, a contagious *saudade*.

Sorry, Dacosta, I said, but I have to leave this dream, the Portuguese Nun is terrifying, I think she might do something desperate while her lover's off enjoying his summer on a beach in Provence.

Wait now, Dacosta answered, we still have to visit her heart, we have to get to the bottom of her desire.

He took me by the hand and said: just a few steps more, one to see the

*Coração*, another to see *A* árvore *dos corações*, the third to see *Três cora*ções *à moda do Minho*.

I took three steps, I followed him and found myself inside the hearts of the Portuguese Nun. These hearts were like night, shrouded in darkness and mystery. A tree bore them as fruit, but they were somber as sin. Trembling, I said: please, Dacosta, can we please leave this dream, the hearts of the Portuguese Nun make my own heart ache, I can't bear these hearts of darkness, you're so brave, sir, how do you manage to be so brave?

Who knows, said Dacosta, maybe because I've spent so many years thinking about dreams, maybe because I've spent so many years thinking only about hearts of darkness.

And what were you doing all those years? I asked, sorry to be so nosy, but I'd really like to know what you were doing.

I was thinking, Dacosta answered, just thinking, and having visions, it's hard to endure your own thoughts and visions for years on end, but I did.

Well, I said, I just can't bear these hearts of darkness, like I said, they make my heart ache, please, take me someplace sunnier, back to your islands, please, let's find a different dream.

Dacosta took hold of my hand and said: that's easy enough, *Açoriana*'s right here, a few steps away, it's a four-part dream, maybe we can stop for dinner.

We stopped on a beach. A beach on one of my islands, Dacosta said, look how pretty it is.

The beach, of fine golden sand, was sprinkled with shellfish, mollusks, and small blue concretions that seemed to come from another planet. There was a wooden beach hut painted white, and on the door was scrawled: Restaurant. We went inside and Dacosta greeted the host. He was a strange host, with a pair of blue wings on his back and a shock of red hair. This is my *Caça ao anjo*, Dacosta said, that's the name of this restaurant, and this is my guardian angel, the angel who looks after my stomach and my soul.

The host bowed, flapped his wings, and asked me: so, do you like red-haired angels?

Yes, indeed, I answered, I've never met one before, but here in the Azores, there seem to be a lot of strange beings, might you by any chance come from another planet?

I come from Saturn, the angel said, everyone thinks we're all saturnine and gloomy on Saturn, and instead we've got blue wings and red hair – but it's not the Saturn you're thinking of – it's the Saturn that Dacosta dreams. And while he walked toward the kitchen he said: I'll fix you up a nice dish, something from the ocean, I've sailed a long time in the ocean of space with my blue wings.

Dacosta looked at me and smiled, and uncorked a bottle of *vinho de cheiro*. Maybe you'd like to learn a bit more, he said. You want to hear about my Saturn?

I admitted I would. Dacosta poured me a glass of wine and said: I have a Saturn I've thought about for years, it's the idea of Saturn – not the planet – it's the God who oversees the birth of the gods, and I've always been pursued by this Saturn; for years and years, while I was preoccupied with my dreams, he was always there, in my heart and spirit, and I'd hear his voice telling me that one day the gods would be born, would burst forth in me, and that day I would be happy.

And how did you respond to your Saturn? I asked.

I kept quiet, Dacosta said, and I waited. And then one day the gods started to be born, this sort of thing usually takes place in spring, but this was fall, I started feeling sick, my soul swelled like the sea swells at the equinox, I went to bed with a cup of herbal tea and waited to give birth. Then at some point I got up, went over to my easel, took up my palette and brushes, and traced two lines on the canvas, two curved lines, like a fountain, because I knew this was my geometric shape. And the gods came on their own, I started painting, and I was happy. And I painted a number of pictures, in a state of ecstasy I can't describe. That was my day of triumph, and I'll never have another one like it.

The angel arrived at our table with an enormous platter of food, something unusual, sumptuous-looking. I asked what it was. This ancient dish, the angel said, was once cooked here, in lost Atlantis, and now I've made it for you.

While we ate, Dacosta requested water, but specifically from the Sintra fountain, the one with two ice-cold jets of water, in the restaurant courtyard. That was odd. That seemed strange, a *Fonte de Sintra* on that Azore island.

Want to see a cave? Dacosta asked me, I know a cave, here in Sintra, where two sirens live.

He pushed a shrub aside, and I saw *Duas serias à boca de uma gruta*: two girls, pink in color, were embracing and tenderly kissing each other on the mouth. Their slender aquatic tails, entwined, created a plant-like cushion. The sirens waved for us to enter. Inside was a table of shells and a seaweed sofa. We sat down and the two sirens told us they'd just spent their afternoon at Praia das Maçãs, lying on the shore. We were

*Duas sereias ao sol na praia*, they said in unison, and we made a liqueur from Praia das Maçãs apples, a liqueur that aids in dreams and serves as a guide in the realm of delirium, and it's what you both need tonight.

They offered us two conch shells filled with amber liqueur, I drank and felt a terrific sadness wash over me. Because I now found myself in a *Paisagem da Terceira*, and it was dawn, midday, and dusk all at the same time. I started sweating, and I thought: this is a hallucination, I'm in one of my own novels. I looked for Dacosta but didn't see him, and this made me more anxious. I took a few steps, searching for him, then saw a wall that split the landscape into two landscapes, and I heard Dacosta's voice. This is my *Melancolia*, he said, I've hid behind melancolia, I'm speaking to you from here, from my melancolia.

The wall that split the landscape in two had a round electric switch halfway up, or maybe it was the button off a lost jacket, who can say. In the foreground, to the left, a cat was sleeping, and in the background you could see castle walls and a woman carrying a baby. On the right was a ruin, maybe an old mill, some sight in the Azores, I couldn't say where. Dacosta jumped down from the wall splitting the landscape. I was straddling the wall, he said. I was straddling my melancolia.

What year is this? I asked.

It's 1942, Dacosta answered, the Second World War isn't over, I'm living in the Azores, far from Europe, and in the distance I can hear the echoes of the slaughter. I'm a young painter, I spend my days walking around my island, and I paint and experience the melancholy of distance and war.

And what are you reading, Dacosta? I asked.

Oh, he said, Bergson and Kafka mainly. With Bergson, I get the melancholy of time and with Kafka, the melancholy of the absurd. And so I painted this dream with my mother in the distance, and she's cradling me in her arms, and there's my cat, my melancholy cat, who's followed me around my entire life. But before that, there's more metaphysical melancholy, he said, my dream about thinking – do you see it? – This is *O filósofo*. He showed me the bust of a classical figure with his brain showing, and beside the bust, a key hung on a nail. Dacosta smiled. This key, he said, is the key to understanding. My philosopher understood Science, he understood Art, he understood God. But he never managed to understand Life. So he hung the key on the nail and started meditating so fervently that his brain grew and grew and broke through his skull and now shows on the outside. See him meditating, he's deep in his meditative sleep; his eyes are wide open, but he's staring at the Truth.

Let's not disturb him, I said. We should leave him be, I'd like to visit some other dream, no, actually, could you please take me to a specific dream of yours?

Dacosta winked at me and said: you need a little music, I've prepared a musical finale for you, a *Serenata açoriana*, but it's not a real serenata, it's a musical piece typical of the Azores, that's called *Sapateira*, a scene filled with melancholy, one of my first hearts of darkness.

Dacosta took a step forward, and I followed. I found myself standing in front of a dying, naked woman. Her body was burning red, perhaps from grief, and a heavy chain was wrapped around her neck. A youth, his expression ironic, was offering her a dead bird, a seagull maybe, who could say. It was night, and while there was no moon, the scene was bright and clear. You could see a woman rowing across a bay and in the background was a house. I knew that house. It was the home of the Woman of Porto Pim. So we're in Faial, I thought, and that woman crossing the water was the Woman of Porto Pim, searching for her whaler. I shivered and said: Dacosta, I'm confused, sorry, but I know that's the Woman of Porto Pim, what's she doing in your dream? Dacosta gave me a seemingly indulgent smile. My dear friend, he said, you came to the Azores in the early '80s and you thought you discovered a story. But I already knew that story back then. I met the Woman of Porto Pim and never told you, remember that night when we had dinner at the home of Hellmut and Alice in Colares? – you told me that story and gave me your book as a gift, but you're naïve, my friend, I'm sorry to have to tell you, but I already knew all those stories, I appreciated your enthusiasm and naïveté, and that's why I became your friend.

And this serenata of yours, I said, that the Portuguese Surrealists of that period were so crazy for – all those enthusiastic, liberal young artists who created Surrealism in Portugal and took it as their manifesto – but what did they actually understand about this dream of yours?

Dacosta grew pensive. I couldn't say, he answered, maybe they loved its magic or its sense of defeat. They were damned from the start, but they still fought the good fight, they wanted to make a difference in life, but those times were too hard for someone wanting to make a difference in life. Literature, you know, can't make a difference in life.

So where do you suppose life is? I asked.

Well, Dacosta answered, life is always elsewhere – that's what the French poet used to say. But now we've come to the end of my dream, it's time for you to go back to your own dreams. He held out his hand, and I shook it. Goodbye, Dacosta, I said, I hope we'll see each other again in some other dream.

So do I, Dacosta said and walked off. I stood watching him fade away on the horizon. The landscape grew opaque, a veil lowered over the scene.

Till the next Azores, I called. He turned around and waved. And just then, I heard the voice of Caterina Bueno singing: "I had a pony, all dappled gray, who counted phases of the moon…"

# On the Road to Möbius

They ask us to identify ourselves. It's mandatory, they say, otherwise, there's no crossing the border; over here, you have to be identifiable. We Humans need to identify everything, we create records, have expansive archives, sorry, but please fill out the questionnaire and provide your papers; identify yourselves, then, that's the idea; I don't know how you say it in your language, they tell us.

Okay, okay, Mr. Human, sometimes we have one ear, and sometimes none, it all depends, not to be disrespectful, I swear, but we hear each other perfectly fine, it's just that sometimes it's our nature to leave out the particulars, perhaps that's hard for you to understand, our nature's not as normative as yours, it does its best, you know, it's been in the same business a long while, much longer than yours has, believe me, millions and millions and millions of – what's the word – years? No, we don't measure with that sort of unity, I was saying millions of millions of millions, and maybe that's boring, I mean, even nature gets bored, there's a monotony to the Universe, that's it, maybe our nature's been caught up in this monotony, and then there's something else to consider, I understand you all classify us as being exceptions, you arrange according to the exception, but with us, you see, this would be impossible, because we only have the exception and not the rule, and it's not a general exception, which for you, would be a kind of rule: it's an individual exception, each of us being an exception per se, so according to your criteria, our nature isn't based on completeness: it's based on approximation. If I may, though, I'd like to pose a question: are all of you so certain you're based on completeness? Perhaps five fingers are less complete than six? Are five fingers more complete than three?

As you can see, though, we forced ourselves to be like you. I'm not saying we forced ourselves to assume your likeness: that might seem arrogant, like undue appropriation, a punishable offense for you. And we're well aware that those who tend to be like you are seen as possible rivals who might replace you; that's not our intention, I promise, and I speak for all my kind: ours is a form of professed and open imitation. We're like your gods who came down among you and assumed your likeness, always, in every age, in every religion you practice. But they were too divine to be truly human. As you can see, we're satisfied with a vague resemblance, but our aim is substance over form, or rather, the *inside* over the *outside*. Here's an example: eyes. We're interested in what's *inside* the eyes. No, it's hard to explain, I don't mean what's *inside*, I mean what's *behind*. Let's just say that when it comes to eyes, we're interested in what's *behind* them. Look at me, for instance. Over on your side, it's common to say: look into my eyes. But I'd rather say: look *beyond* my eyes. Go on, try. To understand each other, it will take considerable effort on both our parts, and also some faculties not listed on this questionnaire of yours, where everything's so instantly describable, so concrete, so limited. I see eye color listed here. So everyone marks off: black, blue, green, brown, even yellow, like a cat. But do you think that's all there is to understanding eyes? The faculties for true understanding, for making a real effort, don't show up on this questionnaire. And yet these are faculties that serve you daily, that you often rely on. Why not try using these faculties when considering my eyes? How so? Well, try using your imagination, for instance. Through your imagination, your eyes could penetrate my eyes, could read what's behind them, am I making myself clear? That's it – some of you, I see, are beginning to understand – to see. Actually, you're not in such unchartered territory, I wonder what strange sights you're frightened of at first, what remote planets with their alien creatures creeping about, their freakish anatomy so foreign to your own harmonious nature. And instead, look, here's a beautiful, austere building and a lovely garden surrounded by an elegant wrought-iron fence – look at all the flowers – Sunday the visiting bishop praises the Monsignor director and the gardeners, oh, such fine religious gentlemen to concern themselves with these children, the ladies who bring candy at Christmas comment on all the children in the world who don't get to have candy, but the children living in this beautiful home get to have candy, and most of all, they get to keep warm in the winter, but today's a beautiful spring day and in that garden is a tree with a swing where two children sit and these two are close friends even if they are so young, they're friends because they've been told they're brothers, even if they are different colors, and they're swinging together, taking turns pushing off and stretching their legs out, toward the future, as your poet who loves lyricism might say, so all right – toward the future, the future, which is present, here in these eyes you're looking into, a present that depends on that past spring day, because then a male voice is calling from the building, ordering them to go inside, it's an authoritative voice, and there's no disobeying, because you can't disobey grownups, and besides this is the Monsignor's voice, and the Monsignor is a stern man, he insists on prayer and obedience; Monsignor wears a cilice, and when the children hear him calling, they feel like crying because darkness and punishment bring on tears. But there's no need to continue, you already know this. Now do you understand what it means to read beyond the eyes?

The eyes control the mouth, you might find this strange, but it's mainly true, at least in your case. Because the mouth often serves to bring out what's entered through the eyes. You know, we're jealous of how your mouth functions. Not that it's a cure, I'll admit that, not that it's a cure at all, what happened, happened and can't be cured with a voice. It's only a palliative, but it's certainly better than nothing. Yes, a howl is certainly better than nothing. But when the mouth can't be used to howl, when it's only a dark tunnel where the beast bellows in silence, you'll realize it's a different mouth. It's mouth-like, what we've assumed in your likeness, so we can be among you, so you'll accept us, really, out of pure sympathy, and we'd like this sympathy to be valued. Because, as I was saying, we're satisfied by a vague resemblance and if we say *ecce homo*, the trunk is laid bare, we wear a crown of fireflies and you can see on your own how hard it is for us to become emperors or female popes or rise to other high offices that you admire and kneel down to. For god's sake, no bowing – not that – we're the ones who should be bowing down to you, and this is why we're willing to fill out your questionnaire.

At times, we're pregnant with ourselves, a self-sufficient way of being, what little there is to us. Because, unlike you, we know these likenesses are fleeting: while you always think you're so much like yourselves that you're eternal, and then when you disappear, you feel bad about it. Or you leave others confused. But not us, we're ready to dissolve, one "poof" and the air we're made of blurs with the surrounding air, as the dream vanishes when the dreamer awakes. That's it – you disappear when you fall asleep. While we disappear when you wake up. Careful, though: we're not dreams, we only have the same nature.

What should be our place of origin on this questionnaire you want us to fill out? We could say we're from the stellar regions, but that wouldn't be precise. Let's use astronomical terms, though, so you can understand, in the end, it's always a matter of the abyss: let's just say we're from the unchartered territories that astronomers call black holes but that you carry within yourselves. And so, to you, we're millions of light years away, yet at the same time, we're beneath your skin, we're your *inside* that's now on the outside, watching you. We're your pattern, in a way, your imprint, your beginning. And possibly your end as well, but who can say.

Oh, almost human brothers who, like us, are only hanging by an air thread! If I could, I'd embrace you all, in this respite of yours, before you return to your beginnings. Almost human brothers, your life's so strange, and stranger still is how you measure it, like a geometric segment with an actual length of time. You even have your scientists who rejoice when that segment increases, who draw up their statistics and never guess it's only a brief spark in the absolute vortex of Everything. Come to think of it, we don't need your passport, we were only filling out your mandatory questionnaire to be polite. Really, you should be filling out your own questionnaire, but with different questions: the ones you've come up with aren't of much use. We don't have any border to cross. How about you?

# An Unforgettable Night

…They saw a dog, but that had to be a different day, who knows when, late in their life together, anyway. The dog's name was Vanda – not with a w, just a v, a begging mutt like that. The dog didn't tell them its name, it couldn't, it couldn't even pant any more, but Rosamunda remembered, when she saw the dog up ahead. Look, a dog – it's Vanda – you remember? They almost hit her – it was dark in the tunnel and they were rounding a curve. Once out of the tunnel, on the straightaway, they pulled to the side to wait, to avoid being rear-ended by a truck, which can happen. Vanda appeared, limping along, head drooping, tongue down to the asphalt, but she was off to the right, well clear of the white line. Her teats swung low, like she'd been nursing, nursing a litter, though this wasn't possible: just from her lips and teeth, she looked to be at least twenty, even older, which was fine for a person but decrepit for a dog. It's because she's so kindhearted, one of them said, I don't remember who, Vanda's good, a good girl, she's spent her life buried up to the neck. They hauled her onto the back seat, the pads of her paws were raw from her journey. They knew she'd gone hundreds of kilometers for them to find her, though they didn't say it, some things you just don't say; a being has to drill through layers and layers of time, pulling around itself the bits and pieces necessary for it to take shape, until it breaks the surface, a living creature, though perhaps already dying, like Vanda, so fucked from the start, thinking it's about to start, when it's already on the way out. Christ, he said, what's the point? A rhetorical question… It was noon and very hot and the sun was blinding – the Mediterranean sun. When things like this happen, it's always very hot, the sun's always blinding, and it has to be Mediterranean – that's a well-known fact. So well-known, you can believe it or not, your choice. And if you feel like believing it, at the moment he was driving slowly, the rocky coast stretched out, reddish, the strip of sea, a deep blue. Vanda seemed to be sleeping, but she wasn't, she had one eye closed, one eye open, fixed upon the back car door and the ashtray full of butts, as if this ashtray were the meager aleph she'd been granted and in this universe of butts, she might discover the sick god who'd created her, the sinister mysteries of his religion. Glancing back at her, he could see the question in her fearful eye, the pupil dilated, and he whispered, the father's a dark turn, the son's those spat-out cigarette butts, and the holy spirit's a time long gone by now – there's your holy trinity, dear Vanda, accept your fate – there's nothing you can do. You never wanted children, Rosamunda said, and she seemed to be speaking to the slight haze of heat dancing on the horizon, all those years, your sperm always left on my belly, thrown away, and now my Vanda's been born, but it's late, too late. She'll die tomorrow, he said, but keep her tonight, rock her like she's your child, offer her your breast, if you want, it's better than nothing, I threw my sperm away because you lied, so I lied, too. . . What a strange night, in Taddeo's *Zimmer*. Framed by the window, two ships sliding by, lit up, silent, dreamlike. Only afterwards, when the ships had moved beyond the frame, did they catch a handful of notes on the wind, weak notes, maybe a waltz. Were they dancing on board? Not out of the question: there's often dancing on board a ship, especially on a cruise, even a short, cheap Sunday cruise like the one that crosses from San Fruttato to San Zaccarino and lasts for only a day. As soon as they can, the people on board start dancing, you have to take advantage of the time you have to enjoy yourself, especially if you bought the ticket, because Monday comes soon enough. Rosamunda tried to offer Vanda her breast, but she wouldn't nurse. They heard her weak breathing almost till dawn, then it stopped. They buried her there, on the beach, in a pocket-sized cove full of pebbles where a path drops down to the water's edge, the small waves washing over pebbles, over them again, century after century. With shells and small stones, Rosamunda spelled out Vanda zero zero zero zero on the grave, those zeros referring to the day she was born and the day she died, and also, as Tristano alone would know, filling them with the time gone by from the day Rosamunda had begun to desire a child to that day when her desire had been buried beneath the body of an old dog, because bit by bit, desires also die and wind up buried underground. They stayed to watch the sun rise over that sliver of horizon between two promontories, in that charming seaside resort, which they'd been to other times by bus. The sun was quite strong, and they both understood without speaking, because everything under the sun is old, sometimes very old. Which doesn't diminish anyone's suffering, including theirs.

Sing me something, she said softly, like you used to. Like what? he asked. Like when we were up in the mountains and you carried me on the handlebars of your bicycle, and you sang to me, remember? I leaned my head on your chest and while you sang, I caught whiffs of garlic – we ate so much garlic in the mountains! – but maybe that was another time, when we ate escargot à la provençal, we'd eat escargot à la provençal, we'd treat ourselves, and those were full of garlic, too.

He sang, the olive falls, no leaves fall, your beauty won't ever, you're like the sea of waves that grows with wind, but with water, never. It was a lullaby. Hard to say if it was to rock Vanda toward her final nothing, or if it was for them, or for their never-ending dreams.

# Hold it – Don't Wake Up

He seemed to brush away a fly. He was quiet. His hands had stopped smoothing out the creases in his trousers. Eyes closed, head back against the chair cushion, he looked like he'd fallen asleep. Many years ago, he whispered, I kept having this dream, it started when I was fifteen, in the camp, and for half my life it was always there, a night seldom went by that I didn't have that dream, the truth is, it wasn't really a dream because dreams – even the most disjointed – still tell a story, and mine was only an image, like a photo, no, it was my head that snapped the photo, if I can put it that way, because I was standing there, staring into the fog, and at some point, click, my brain snapped the photo and there in front of me this landscape evolved, no, it wasn't any landscape, it was a landscape made up of nothing, there was mainly a gate, a magnificent white gate, thrown open onto a landscape that wasn't there, and that's all there was to that image, the dream was mainly how I felt while I stared at this image that my brain had photographed, because dreams aren't so much what happens as the emotion you feel as it happens, and I couldn't really tell you about the emotion I was feeling because emotions aren't explainable, to explain them, you have to turn them into feelings, as Baruch knew, but a dream isn't the right place to turn emotion into feeling, I can tell you it was quite the torment for me, because while I felt a strong desire to take off running, to fly through that wide-open gate, to plunge into the unknown beyond and escape toward what I couldn't say, I also felt a sense of shame, like guilt for something I didn't do, and the fear of hearing my father's voice accusing me, but there was no voice in that dream, it was a voiceless dream, with the fear of hearing a voice.

# A Discovered Letter

To Monsieur François Dominique Arago
Académie des Sciences
Paris

Universe, January 1, 1840

Mister Physicist, Mister Astronomer,

You don't know the nature of matter, you don't know the nature of antimatter. In your meager scientist's laboratory, you think you've captured the secrets to the universe. Combining hydrogen and oxygen in your cruets, you think you understand the secrets to water. Peering through your microscope at the infinitely small workings of our body, you think you understand the secrets to life. Peering through your telescope at the infinitely distant, you think you understand the secrets to the stars. But the elements of the universe, mister scientist, aren't composed for your lenses. Water, Air, Earth, Fire: these hold secrets you may never understand. The stars follow a path you find unfathomable. And do you know why? Because they dance. Everything dances, mister scientist, and you're not allowed to follow this dance. And do you know why everything dances? Because, mister scientist, everything is music, and everything in its turn obeys a music that your ears can't grasp. Air, Water, Earth, Fire are all music. And they dance the music that they themselves are. The life you're searching for in your laboratory, in your observatory, is a music you will never grasp.

Yet there is a way for you to grasp the meaning of life, if only briefly. But this music won't be grasped through sound – it will be through silence. Because music, as you well know, isn't, and couldn't be, continuous sound. It's also made up of silences: miniscule intervals, pauses between one sound and the next, one note and the next; incalculable gaps where life stops only to resume again, this pulse which to us seems steady. Here it is, then: regarding the music of life, this magical way I've mentioned grasps the fleeting interval, the gap invisible to the naked eye, the silence already drained of before and brimming with after. And renders it eternal. I'm speaking of photography, something I'm very familiar with, since I discovered a process for making photographs more vivid and clear. But you stole my process and gave it to your friend Daguerre. You are the cause of my deathly despair. But my despair will also be your regret, sent to you here in the form of two photographs.

In the first, you'll find me in front of my country cottage, in the exact place where I left behind my human features. Then I went down to the creek where, in the summertime, I'd go and photograph flowers and the delicate dragonflies alighting briefly on the surface of the water. I walked into the creek and surrendered to its embrace. I left my corpse by the door, exactly how I'd photographed myself five minutes before, and then I went to photograph my ethereal body, which in the meantime had flown off to the stars. You may ask how this marvel could be carried out. Well, it's simple: with your telescope, by applying an invention of mine to that instrument, which this time you won't be able to steal, because I won't tell you what it is. You'll search in vain with your instrument, in your Parisian nights, scanning the stars in hopes of discovering a yet unknown constellation to render your name forever famous. But the only star you'll discover and regret will be me. You'll search for me in Orion's belt, while I sleep forever, emanating my steady starlight: you'll see me with my head resting serenely against the darkness of the universe, and my face will hold the superior, distant expression of one chosen for the heavens. No matter how hard you try, you won't see another star beyond me, and your foolish astronomer's name will be forever linked to mine. This will be your only claim to fame, my sad little scientist, that in the entire universe, you only discovered one new celestial body: the Hippolyte Star.

This is the revenge of a clown from a family of celestial clowns, with my head in the stars and my feet in the grave.

Farewell,
Hippolyte Bayard

# Double Enigma

The writer was staring at those stones and thinking: what is a stone? After a while he decided a stone is a stone is a stone is a stone. All right. But maybe a stone means something? No: a stone *in and of itself*, like a tree *in and of itself*, doesn't mean a thing. And where were those stones, anyway? In the air, like four-sided stars dancing in the cosmos? In the painter's heart? In his life? In the dramatic moment in the life of Alberto Magnelli (the painter he was looking at) – and was this really why he'd started drawing stones?

He was reminded of a poem, from more or less this same period, that also included stones. It was written in '22, he remembered this clearly because he heard it read in São Paulo's *Semana de Arte Moderna*. He'd memorized it in translation, and now, remembering, he said it out loud:

*In the middle of the road there was a stone*
*there was a stone in the middle of the road*

> *there was a stone*
> *in the middle of the road there was a stone.*

> *I shall never forget this event*
> *in the life of my tired retinas.*
> *I shall never forget that in the middle of the road*
> *there was a stone*
> *there was a stone in the middle of the road*
> *in the middle of the road there was a stone.*

His retinas were tired, too, from looking at those solid, sharp-edged stones, because the more he looked, the more ambiguous and fleeting they became, like clouds rolling by on the wind. He thought: the moonstone, the touchstone, the philosopher's stone, the milestone, the Bologna stone.

A stone can be so many things. He sought help from the exegetes. One discussed the marble quarries that the painter, when he left Italy, had carried with him, in his retinas. That sounded like a reasonable explanation: the marble mountains of Carrara where Michelangelo extracted his stones – once you saw those mountains, you'd never forget them. He read another exegesis: Magnelli was influenced by the mountains in "primitive" Tuscan paintings. That seemed reasonable: those were also unforgettable mountains – if you saw those mountains in the Uffizi, you'd never forget them. But why hadn't someone thought about Leonardo and his *Virgin of the Rocks*? There were certainly stones in that one, too. Maybe when he abandoned Italy, Magnelli decided out of a sense of consideration to leave the Virgin's ineffable smile in place and carry away only her stones. A dilettante's exegesis, but still, it did sound reasonable. Tricky, those stones. The more he looked, the more of an enigma they seemed.

He thought he'd consult Drummond de Andrade, the poet who'd found a stone in the middle of the road which had stayed with him, in his tired retinas. He had the poet's complete works in the original Aguilar edition, but the one he wanted now was the French edition for the Parisian gallery that had asked him to contribute a piece. He looked for it in his library. He started flipping through it, hoping the curator had included the work he needed. And luckily, there it was, a *poème en prose*, titled *L'Enigme*. So he translated it for himself from the original.

### The Enigma

The stones were walking down the road. When suddenly, a
dark form blocked their way. They mused on this, based on
their own experience. They were familiar with other moving
forms and knew the dangers of every object that went about
the earth. This form, however, in no way fit what they'd seen
in their limited lives, these prisoners of habit, crushed beneath
a stone's mindless instinct. The stones halted. In their effort to
understand, they froze. And concentrating on this moment,
they remain forever fixed in place, to form colossal mountains or
only stunned, bewildered, wretched rocks.

He felt greatly relieved. The *poème* included a second part, but he already had his answer here, because this was how poets solved the enigmas of life: by representing them with other enigmas, just like Oedipus, who solved the enigma of the Sphynx only to have the enigma of life waiting for him on the other side.

He was about to put the book back when his glance fell on the most recent musings of the exegetes on the painter's stones. There on the glowing screen, encyclopedic Mister Google was calling to him. Good lord, what about Nietzsche? How had he managed to forget about Nietzsche, especially *The Dawn*, as Mister Google suggested? Maybe because it was nighttime, the gallery was expecting his piece and had already left him two messages, so he felt hurried? In their static state, stones don't tolerate hurried conversation. But Nietzsche's words seemed absolutely perfect for this critic's idea about Magnelli: that words are stones and their dead weight blocks – chokes – communication. And so the critic concluded that Magnelli used those stones to depict a petrified Italy, the totalitarian, fascist state he'd managed to free himself from. This was more than reasonable. The Drummond enigma, by which he believed he may have solved the enigma of the stones, vanished like mist in sunshine. While at the same time Magnelli's stones, as if offended by the light, slipped back into the shadow of their enigma. Then he opened Drummond's book again and read the second part of that *poème en prose*:

*But the mysterious Thing – itself enormous – still remains, as enigmas do, mocking all attempts at interpretation. It is the curse of enigmas that they can't decipher themselves. They lack the insight of others, which could free them from the curse of their confusion. But at the same time they disavow this insight, for such is the condition of enigmas. This halts the advancing stones – gullible flock – and tomorrow it will stop the trees from moving, save on windy days; and*

*it will stop the birds; and the air teeming with insects and vibrations;*
*and each and every life; and the universal capacity to agree and to*
*conclude that survives in every conscience. The enigma tends to*
*paralyze the world.*

But then, he wondered, if the enigma tends to paralyze, what can be done? He went back to reading the poem.

*The enormous Thing might suffer to its very fibers, but lacks*
*compassion for itself and for those it reduces to impending ice.*
*Oh, what good is intelligence! the stones complain. We were once*
*intelligent – considering a threat won't eliminate that threat, but*
*creates it. Oh, what good are feelings! the stones complain. We were*
*sensitive once, but the gift of mercy turned on us when we planned*
*to bestow it on those less fortunate. [...] But the interceptor Thing is*
*still unmoved. It blocks the road and ponders, darkly.*

This time, he felt he'd found the answer to the enigma. Because if the Thing blocks the road and ponders, darkly, then into that darkness the artist steps forward, like a miner steps forward into a mine, a light shining from his forehead. Forward, artist. But toward what? And why?

le minotaure                    Adam  ahmedabad  1.1.96

# The Minotaur's Headaches

*Borges and Dürrenmatt were suspicious of the Minotaur's depression, but in the end, perhaps it wasn't for them to understand his illness, the course of the venous and arterial blood, the imponderable tides of serotonin. A condition, a poet once wrote, that only the privileged few experience, those familiar with the headache and the universe.*

*Daedalus was the first to witness these terrible headaches. He knew that fracturing space into a grid of a thousand right angles, the way a fly's eye would see it, thwarts Euclid's true intentions, reducing his precise geometry to a meaningless, panic-inducing fractal. As it scans and tries to decipher, the optic nerve, which Euclid was attuned to, sends conflicting messages to the cerebral cortex, each message denying the one that came before. One angle leads to freedom, another to eternal prison: but they're equal and com-plimentary, jeering Siamese twins of stone that no goniometer could ever measure.*

The labyrinth that day was shrouded in heat. Daedalus wandered its passageways, exhausted, searching for a place where the suffocating ceilings might break open even a little so he could look beyond the unsurmountable walls and catch a glimpse of blue sky. Over his shoulder he carried a sack of beeswax and feathers. He suddenly found himself in a large chamber he didn't recall, with frescos of graceful, reddish figures bearing gifts and dancing in a frenzy. On a stone bench covered in pillows, the young monster sat clutching his head. Tears ran down from his great bovine eyes to soak his slender chest. Seeing him, Daedalus felt moved by pity. Why are you crying, boy? he asked. You know why, the Minotaur answered, you're the only one who knows what brings on a vision of the universe, and you've locked me away in the outline of its image. Daedalus was silent, and the boy went on: do you know what a headache means? Not a migraine, not a slight headache – there are potions to make those pass. This is something much worse, much different: a multifaceted event occurring inside our head and soul. And it's not easy explaining something that's many different things at once. First, it's a small noise, that's how it starts. But it's not something you hear, it's like a bell that rings and doesn't ring, and you hear it all the same: like a hiss. Or a whistle? Or a whine? Something like these but going on and on. In short: a call. Something calling from afar, from deep deep down. And you can feel it. And then suddenly, ferociously, edges rise. That imposter hiss that's come in silence now violates your vision, heightens it: edges, corners are expanding now, as though you're seeing objects swell up in space, and these objects mean something different than they did before, something this expansion has conferred upon them: they've changed form, now they're melting.

The Minotaur stopped and clutched his head, then scraped it against the wall, like a wounded animal. Go on, Daedalus said.

The Minotaur sighed. You see that wardrobe against the back wall and that mirror over there, with the big, stupid fly batting against it? They're a wardrobe and a mirror, and you'll always see them as a wardrobe and a mirror, that's all they'll ever mean. Then suddenly they aren't what they are anymore, they're simply an expression of lines and volumes occupying a space. That wardrobe becomes a cube, and you understand it as a cube, the same way you did when the mathematician at school set a solid object down on a bench so you could draw its geometric projection. Because a cube is a cube, not a wardrobe – do you see? Sitting there in front of you, it's abstract, an idea, and nothing more, just a set of lines. And now everything is swaying, the tide of space is swelling, shrinking, and you're on top and swaying at its mercy, you have to sit, you might roll onto the ground, this fluid ground that can't keep you steady on your legs, your two legs when you need four at least, you can feel it, you want to be on four legs but you're on your last two instead, and around you, no, *inside you,* there breathes a cavernous lung that seems like the universe, and you're on top and inside at the same time, you're a miserable speck tossing about in the alveoli of this monstrous lung that's breathing in and breathing out. Chronos, Uranus – that sort of lung – one that gnaws on you, devours you, and you press on your temples, you bear down, holding back that tide of time bursting in your head like a boiling, primordial soup, where you drown. This, Daedalus, is a headache. Do you realize what you've condemned me to?

# A Midwinter Night's Dream

Was the moon up? Yes, the moon was up. A murderer wanted to kill the moonlight, but hadn't succeeded. And the moonlight flooded the white of white. And the hamlet slept. It was a hamlet of only a few ancient, dark houses. The only light came from one small window. Not lamplight, firelight, and a man sat in front of a fireplace, legs stretched over the stones near the andirons. He was watching the sparks, what his grandfather (back in the day) called, "the little girls," for how they danced and sparkled like eyes. The "little girls" soared up, into the dark of the chimney. The man turned toward the window and saw the white slowly coming down and thought: snow, soot. Then he thought of a haiku he heard long ago, in a distant city, and the woman singing it to him in her sweet voice:

> *I unfold my paper cloak*
> *and step outside*
> *to watch the snow.*

And he felt himself overcome by sleep, and he slowly rose, as if taking flight; he unfolded a paper cloak, put it on, and opened the door. But how charming this paper cloak was, he only realized it now, and how strange: the landscape painted on it was the same view framed by the doorway, barely visible now in the dark: a blanket of white with variations of white, a blanket, mysteriously white, invitingly white, and covering the landscape like a cloak. I'm wearing a cloak, the man said, stepping forward into the sooty dark looming over the white; and only then did he notice that this dark wasn't solid or singular, it was composed of shades that went along with the shades of white. What am I looking for? he asked himself. He wasn't sure, but he felt he should advance further into the dark and into the white, so he took a few more steps into the landscape, ah,

> *a dog barks*
> *someone walking by*
> *night of snow.*

There was a stone in the middle of the road, beneath the white. He struck it with his wooden clog, and the sound rang in the night. The dog grew quiet, then went back to barking, faraway, beyond the row of cypresses, on the opposite hill. So that white hid stones – of course – with his eyes adjusting to the shades of black, he could also make out the shades of white. In one, he saw a stone. So what was this snow, then, that had fallen to cover a landscape where (in the shades of black) he now saw the silhouette of a small shrine? Maybe it's some sort of pardon, he thought, that's why the snow fell. But a pardon presupposes suffering, and on this night stroll of his, he was taking part in that pardon, both in the giving and in the receiving of it, and he thought, too, that he had to find the right person for this exchange to occur, and this was why he'd stepped out into the white night. Oh,

> *first snow*
> > *how to sing your praises?*
> > > *moon on bamboo.*

Are you so sure you'll find the person you're looking for? asked a menacing night voice inside him. Of course, he answered frankly, because

> *for the lonely man*
> > *no greater friend*
> > > *the moon.*

The moon, the moon, moonmoonmoon, the moon above isn't concerned with your fate, said the cruel night voice inside him. And suddenly a chasm opened, the landscape tore, cadmium shone on the white, the black turned flamingo, and the lonely man opened his eyes again. The fire had turned to ash, everything was quiet, silence all around and inside him, the house desolate, everything desolate, and he whispered: it was only a dream, no one's coming. But instead,

> *fire buried under ash*
> > *dead of night*
> > > *a knocking.*

*Andantes, con Brio*

# The Heirs are Grateful

*To my friends I leave*
*a cerulean blue for flying high*
*a cobalt blue for happiness*
*an ultramarine blue to stir the spirit*
*a vermilion to make the blood flow allegramente*
*a moss green to ease disquiet*
*a gold yellow: riches*
*a cobalt violet for la rêverie*
*a madder lacquer for the sound of a cello playing*
*a cadmium yellow: science fiction, glitter, splendor*
*a yellow ochre for accepting the ground*
*a Veronese green for remembering spring*
*an indigo for reconciling the spirit to the temporal*
*an orange to practice viewing a distant lemon tree*
*a lemon yellow for grace*

*a pure white: purity*
*a raw sienna: transformation of gold*
*a sumptuous black to see Titian*
*an umber for greater acceptance of regretful black*
*a burnt sienna for the will to endure*

—Maria Helena Vieira da Silva, *Will*

## 1. *Cerulean Blue*

All done, then? Yes, he told himself. Because life ends, and so does poetry. And everyone, dead. How many years since he'd written a poem? And that trip, did it make any sense? There on that terrace overlooking the sea, the same place so long ago, with her…

Summer afternoon. Boredom. Oceanography of boredom. Boredom assumes a seat. And he was seated. Extremely seated. Without his house-keeper, he couldn't rise from his chair. On the table, a pitcher of iced tea seemed to be sitting on the horizon. Below him, the sea; above him, the sky, and that was the moment, on that line between sea and sky, when a small figure appeared, poised, far faraway, then started closer, as if flying in the blue of the air. Here she was. Swimming forward, yes, just like someone swimming forward, and now and then she'd raise her hand as if to say: it's me. And then he took a sheet of the white paper in front of him that had stayed white for years, and he started writing. And he called her snowy egret, perhaps for the nightgown she wore on their wedding night; and cabbage butterfly, perhaps for the sunbeam that briefly veiled her in yellow, like those small butterflies fluttering around the cabbages in our vegetable gardens. And he described her flight in many other ways, in lines that can't be repeated here, because the one doing the telling isn't allowed to repeat them. Until he was done writing; he left the poem beneath the pitcher, rose from his chair with surprising ease, and stepping lightly, like Nijinsky or Nureyev, he moved to the low lime wall at the edge of the terrace and took flight into the cerulean blue, to go and join her.

## 2. *Cobalt Blue*

And then they went and fired him. And his colleague that he always trusted, who stole his files, the files of a reliable executive like her husband, and signed his own name to them instead. What a bastard. She wanted to strangle him with her own two hands. If she could just get a little sleep, lying back against the headrest, while he drove. It would be a good hour before they reached the town where they were staying in a small pensione, on a vacation he'd refused to give up. He'd said: "Come on, don't be like that, we can always sell the house." Sell the house! Six years spent paying for that house, their little house, and now, when it was finally paid off, down to the last centesimo, he'd gone and gotten himself fired for trusting others too much, and he acted like it was nothing: we can always sell the house. Sometimes men were such idiots, no, such babies, men were such big babies. And meanwhile night was falling and she was getting hungry; for lunch they'd only eaten an inedible hotdog. She gave in to the rocking of the curves and closed her eyes. What was that? she asked, his voice waking her. Oh, nothing, he said, I was talking about the sky, look, there, where the light's disappearing – it's cobalt blue. She opened her eyes and looked where he was pointing, and she felt a shiver run through her like an electric jolt, so much so, that she felt a slight tingling in her hands, felt her heart beating, and she asked herself why this feeling had come over her. Was it because they were young? Because it was beautiful being together? Because life was there before them like this road leading down now from the mountains to the sea? Because she wanted a child? Yes, she wanted a child, oh, yes, a child! Was this why she felt so happy? Forgive me, she said, please forgive me. What for? he asked, I don't understand. It doesn't matter, she said, because I do.

### 3. *Ultramarine Blue*

How many years had it been? He started adding them up. Nine, maybe more. When he left he was a boy, and now he was returning. Sure, but where? What did it mean to return? Do you return to the same places? Those places that were ours – are they the same as they once were? A line of poetry came to mind: Do you recognize me, air, you who knew places that once were mine? A German poet wrote that. Or did he still have to write it? That was beside the point, entirely beside the point. He was leaning over the ship's rail, watching the sea. Lisbon was over there, faraway, overseas, in the ultramarine. He told the ship: "Iron ship, don't sail to Port Said! Turn right, where to, I couldn't say." But the ship didn't turn. It just kept sailing straight on. And left a straight furrow of foam in the sea and a straight streak of smoke in the sky. And he said to himself:

it doesn't matter, the only thing to do is make up an imaginary world for yourself where you'll land in a few days, a world all your own that'll seem like it's from your childhood, but it won't be the same as your childhood, because the blue sky's not the same sky from your childhood and everything is irreparably different, you're a sailor returning from a desert island to a made-up continent. He got to work. Because the only thing to do was stir the spirit, and that ultramarine blue was crucial for stirring the spirit. A great painter once said that. Or maybe she still had to say it, but that was beside the point, entirely beside the point.

## 4. *Vermilion*

"…and I was really down, dear, I mean really down – you know – your basic borderline suicidal depressive, and in he walks, a tennis racket under one arm, looking like someone without a care in the world. And at that point I couldn't see straight. I felt my face go vermilion, like when you and I fought when we were girls, and I told him what I'd always wanted to tell him these past twenty years, scalding-hot words, and those words seemed vermilion, too. He just stood there, petrified; he turned white as a corpse and his racket clattered to the floor. And I was filled with such joy, I can't even begin to tell you, it was like I was born again, I could feel the blood flowing through my veins with a force that raised my spirits even more, and I burst out laughing, for the joy of having found joy again, I stood up, trying to control myself, you know, I didn't even take my things, I can always get someone to pick them up if I have to, I just walked out, shut the door behind me, got in the car and left him there, staring at his own navel. Write me soon – at my office address. A hug. Yours."

## 5. *Moss Green*

"…while unlike you, I had to go through the typical autogenic training to regain my composure. Here in Michigan, it's late fall now and the garden's so lovely. On the stone garden bench under the elm tree, moss is growing, soft as silk, a pale, brownish-green color. And believe me, the only thing I've found that calms my nerves is caressing that color. Sorry for the odd expression, you don't caress colors, but I don't know how else to say it, because caressing that moss, I feel like I'm caressing its color. Sometimes I think if you'd married Fred and I'd married Mark, things would have been different, because maybe I liked Mark and you liked Fred. But how is it possible we never realized back then?"

## 6. *Golden Yellow*

"Life, you're beautiful (I say) / you just couldn't get more fecund / more befrogged or nightingaley / more anthillful or sproutsprouting / … / I praise your inventiveness, / bounty, sweep, exactitude, / sense of order – gifts that border / on witchcraft and wizardry."

—Wisława Szymborska could never have written those lines if she hadn't seen Maria Helena Vieira da Silva's golden yellow, this seems perfectly clear, said the first.

—But Maria Helena Vieira da Silva could never have painted that golden yellow, either, if she hadn't read those lines by Wisława Szymborska, you must see this, said the second.

## 7. *Cobalt Violet*

—So listen to this, said the third: "Others will love the things I loved / there'll be the same garden at my door." To reach Maria Helena's golden yellow and Wisława's fecundity, one must have an enormous capacity to dream, no, the inter-dream is necessary, meaning, the *rêverie*. And without question, the *rêverie* is cobalt violet. And if Sophia de Mello Breyner hadn't written these lines, Maria Helena would never have reached her yellow and Wisława, her fecundity.

—That's true, said the other two in unison, however, said one, it's also true that if Sophia had never seen the golden yellow of Maria Helen and never known the richness of Wisława's life, she would never have created the cobalt violet of her *rêverie,* I do hope we can all agree about that.

## 8. *Madder Lacquer*

—Maria Helena, Wislawa, Sophia: three wonderful women, said a voice behind them.

The three friends turned around. It was night, the road was clear. Who said that? Were they hallucinating? But the voice went on:

—When I think about these women, madder comes to mind. You three seem to understand a great deal about colors, so you probably know that madder isn't a solid color, it's a lacquer. In its natural state, madder varies from pink to carmine, but when painted on canvas it turns transparent and makes other colors shine, gleam, magical colors, as if inundated with light, that's why Van Gogh used madder so much when he wanted to capture the light of Provence. Gentlemen, madder lacquer is ethereal, volatile, and it makes colors shine that would otherwise be dull: it's like wearing colored glasses on a gray fall day. Maria Helena, Wislawa, and Sophia are my madder lacquer, and if I look at the world through their eyes I hear a cello playing.

The three friends didn't move. No one dared to speak. There wasn't a living soul in sight. What mystery was this? Then, looking up, they saw an old building, and on the highest floor, light seeping through a half-closed window. A distant window in a mansard roof, and the light wasn't real, it was a transparent halo, a reflection, like madder lacquer. And from that light, they thought they heard the sound of a cello playing. But they were only imagining this, of course.

## 9. *Cadmium Yellow*

He began writing: "And suddenly she appeared to him in the most unexpected places, a brilliant halo surrounding her, a burst of yellow light. It was January, 2082, and scientists had just developed a system for deconstructing the body and reconstructing it at a distance." Not bad for an opening. He thought about the title: *Baryta Yellow*. A nice title, too, for the pseudonym he'd come up with: Phil McPhil.

## 10. *Yellow Ochre*

There was a pale, autumn sun. They all stood around the grave. The gravedigger threw in the first shovelful of dirt. The priest crossed himself and said: "Let us pray that our brother accepts this ochre earth as we shall, and as we accept these yellowing leaves that mark the passing of our seasons."

## 11. *Veronese Green*

"If I had to describe my now distant spring, no, my first springs, I'd think of green. A particular green, though, soaked in nostalgia and desire, and not forgetful of the feelings from back then, like that line from the poet: green, how I want you green. I can't say I know how to define this green exactly, but perhaps what comes the closest is Veronese green."

## 12. *Indigo*

And all around him the storm was blowing, a storm weighing heavy in the atmosphere for days, so much so that the air, the sky, the clouds had all turned indigo, and he stepped off the porch and into the tempest, dancing like a madman in the rain, clutching his fiddle, playing a gypsy tune, dancing and dancing, and his legs, he saw, had also turned indigo, and his arms and hands, and he was dancing and playing the fiddle, and he felt he was a Paganini, a sprig of lavender, a Fellini clown, an eggplant, a turkey, a Chagall fiddler. Because turning to indigo is incredible. An experience reserved for very few.

## 13. *Orange*

That lemon tree was green, and its lemons were yellow, it couldn't be otherwise, but to see it as green with yellow lemons, he had to adjust his vision by starting off at orange; that must seem strange to you, friends, but it's exactly what he had to do: every morning he rose and stared at his lemon tree in the distance, and to see it, he did as someone might who adjusts the wheel of his binoculars to bring an image into focus, only the wheel of his imaginary binoculars rolled according to the color spectrum, and he would start off at orange. That was it exactly: starting off at orange.

## 14. *Lemon Yellow*

She had a grace…I'm not sure I can explain it, a grace…well, an innate elegance to her thoughts and behavior, and a simplicity that only a higher

Grace can give, a grace...how to put it?...a lemon-yellow grace...yes, that's it.

## 15. *Pure White*

"Because pure white is only purity and can only be described as purity, and I write you this while thinking about the snows of Kilimanjaro, and those nights I spent thinking of you. And now, I'm sorry, but I have to go."

## 16. *Raw Sienna*

It was only late, very late, in the Medieval period when an alchemist discovered that sulphurous mineral, found on the slopes of Monte Amiata and in Siena's soil, which gave artists the yellow and all the shades of ochre that classical painters had attempted to create by mixing hues. But no one ever knew this alchemist who'd managed to extract the color called "sienna" from the ground.

The engraver was leaning over his plate where he'd incised a bearded man beside a giant alembic boiling over a wood fire. He could already see the results on paper, the shadowy cave, light beams shooting from the alembic and the alchemist's eyes. He considered a title. Of course, he told himself: *Transformation of gold*. It couldn't be anything else.

## 17. *Sumptuous Black*

The boat plowed through the dark of the lagoon. Venice was near, though he couldn't see it. And not just because it was night: he'd been blindfolded with a black cloth. The peculiar Signore had insisted on this, and he had to obey. He could tell the boat was docking on a pier. Someone took his hand to lead him. They started up a flight of stairs. A voice told him to watch his step: the stones were slippery for someone wearing silk shoes. The stairs ended and a voice told him to take off his blindfold. He obeyed. The palazzo was immersed in even greater darkness. But he knew he was in a great hall, because the dark was soft as velvet, and he could sense all the marvelous tapestries and treasures in the room. The hand still guided him, making him turn back around. Then there came a cry of "light!" and he knew it was the voice of that mysterious Signore. A torch was lit, it glowed against the walls, and then, finally, he stepped from the sumptuous black to see Titian.

## 18. *Raw Umber*

The old Master cleaned his brushes and slipped them into the sake vase like a bouquet. He took the still-damp piece of rice paper and pinned it up over the open window like a curtain. The landscape was no different, only superimposed over the one that was natural: in the foreground, the clump of bamboo in the garden, then the hillsides, the valley with its willow trees, the small lake in the background and the autumn mist rising off the ground and water, into the sky. Even the color was the same, just a little darker, as if approaching nightfall: a raw umber varying by how much he'd diluted the color. But the painted landscape had something the natural landscape didn't: an enormous grasshopper with transparent wing cases, and the bamboo, the hill, the valley, the lake, the mist in the sky were all seen through these wings. His servant girl came in to say that his tea was ready and his bathwater was growing cold. The old Master took off his kimono, folded it and laid it on the mat, he lit the votive lamp for his dead ones, and he stood naked in front of his watercolor, studying it. Then he picked up his ink brush and wrote in the upper right corner, where the raw umber was lightest:

> fall evening
>     regretful black
>         in insect form

### 19. *Burnt Sienna*

"From others, you'll have splendid gifts, I'm sending you this simple honey pot, the honey inside, a deep burnt sienna. The bees that made it come from the mountains where I live, and I extracted the honey. It's for the sweetness you showed me then, to say it still endures and always will."

## 20. *All the Colors*

The man who wrote these stories felt confused and stopped, because he'd made up nineteen characters in order to thank Maria Helena Vieira da Silva for a color she'd left in her will. But for him, the man who wrote these stories, not a single color remained. And this didn't seem fair. So he began to write a little story with a writer as the protagonist who, after writing nineteen stories, each one for one of Vieira da Silva's colors, now wrote a story where he took all nineteen of Vieira da Silva's colors and mixed them into a cocktail, and then he abandoned himself to an incomparable synesthesia. And in that splendid synesthesia, he felt every sensation, every feeling that Vieira da Silva makes one feel with every color. And his story was as simple as simple can be. And this is that story.

# A Difficult Decision

Signora 600 Multipla lay stretched out on her back looking up quizzically at the doctor. Her mouth was open and she was breathing in small puffs. Not really breathing: more of a sputtering rattle, a gurgling that made her body shudder. She tried to gather her remaining strength to whisper: "Am I to be scrap metal, Doctor?"

The doctor smiled and didn't answer right away. His expression grew pensive, to give more weight to his words: "If you don't overdo it, Signora," he said, "if you're willing to lead an extremely sedentary life, then you can go on for a bit yet."

Signora Multipla forced her mouth to smile and closed her eyes. She considered the doctor's strange words, so euphemistic. An extremely sedentary life. That expression translated to *chronically ill*. That's what this young doctor meant, with his evil instruments exploring her guts. Chronically ill. The life of an invalid. She, who'd transported her family everywhere; she, who was so energetic, so patient and hard-working –

now reduced to immobility, to puttering painfully around the garden on Sundays. And her mind turned to better times, to her late husband, the Sunday picnics in the country, the children making such a mess, with her singing, *Only You*. She remembered the trip they'd made to Barcelona. Such fine times!

And how times had changed. All you had to do was look around, to see the other ladies in her neighborhood. An old, traditional neighborhood, now unrecognizable. Especially with that Madame 2CV, who called neighborhood meetings every week, a proletarian acting like a queen. And then there was Diane (she could call her that because she'd known her as a girl), always right there with the other, sputtering and fussing about something, always with her extravagant lipstick and all those decals on her clothes. And then, even worse, was Fräulein Golf. Going either décolleté or extremely sporty, never taking the middle path: as if the world were divided into these two categories. Or Doña Ibiza, that Spanish lady with all her *salero*, who came from some remote suburb of Mancha but made everyone think she had a villa in the Balearic Islands. Not to mention the grandes dames – they were even worse. Take Lady Mercedes, always dressed in black, with that uniformed gentleman who accompanied her everywhere, waiting outside the boutiques while she shopped. And Signora Ferrari, so gaudy, with that high voice of hers. And Signora Thema and her mighty bosom. And, *dulcis in fundo*, onto high society: the Contessa Giulietta-Romeo, for instance, so full of herself, just because some English playwright supposedly talked about her long ago.

Signora Multipla sighed once more, a deep sigh, rusty and willful. "Doctor, I want to be euthanized," she said firmly. The world, she felt, was a vulgar place: pushy, noisy, aggressive. "They can all just go and crash on their awful highways," she thought, "and speed and rear-end each other at stoplights during rush hour!" Dying didn't bother her.

The doctor matter-of-factly detached her valves. Signora Multipla shuddered; from her throat came the squeak of a worn-out toy trumpet, and her heart stopped beating.

# The Lady-with-the-Hat

"Good afternoon," said the Lady-with-the-Hat, "sorry to bother you, but we have to get to Bukhara, and the driver's lost and says it wouldn't be proper for him to speak to you directly, so I need to do the asking, even if you don't understand my language, please excuse me."

The Woman-of-the-Loom smiled broadly, she stepped away from her loom and started blowing on the flames in the brazier beside her door. The Lady-with-the-Hat turned to the taxi driver and gave him a slight wave as if to say: "Your turn – go ahead and translate."

The taxi driver had lowered his window, his elbow protruding now while he stared up at the sky, as if he needed to speak to the clouds. It was a deep blue sky filled with white clouds chasing one another, urged on by the wind. And the enormous field of wheat was filled with wind as well, the ears of ripe wheat bent low on their stalks, then standing upright, like waves on a golden sea crashing against the blue horizon.

It was June, and hot. The Woman-of-the-Loom went back to her loom, smiled again, and spoke in her incomprehensible language, a language that followed a musical scale made up of short and long notes, with rising sharp keys that suddenly dropped in pitch, like a melody. She spoke at length, then returned to her loom.

The Lady-with-the-Hat looked at the taxi driver. "Did you understand where we need to go?"

"She wants to know where you're from," the man answered, still staring into space.

"That's it?" said the Lady-with-the-Hat, "it took all that time just to ask me where I'm from?"

"She wants to know why you're speaking in English even though you're not English – why you don't just speak in your own language."

"And how does she know I'm speaking in English if she doesn't know English?" asked the Lady-with-the-Hat.

"Because she recognizes the sound of English even if she doesn't understand the language," said the driver, staring at the horizon.

"But if she understood I was speaking in English by the sound, how did she figure out that I'm not English?"

"Simple," the driver answered, "she could tell by your tone, English people always order everyone around, even when they're asking for a favor."

The Lady-with-the-Hat smiled, amused, and looked at the Woman-of-the-Loom. "I'm Greek," she said in English, "do you know where Greece is?" And she waited for the driver to translate the Woman-of-the-Loom's answer.

"She wants to know if you want to stay for lunch," the driver answered, "she's lit the brazier for grilling goat sausages with wild herbs because today her grandchildren are coming over."

"But she'd asked me where I'm from," said the Lady-with-the-Hat.

The driver's expression grew condescending, as it might with a tedious child. "First of all, this is a countrywoman, she's certainly not from Samarkand like me, so why on earth would she know where Greece is?" He sighed and calmly lit a very small pipe made of majolica. "I told her you're not English and that's enough, not to mention… Madame, in our country the first thing we do is invite someone to share a meal, especially out in the country, this is basic, your travel guide says so, too – while I drove, all you did was read your guide instead of looking out the window at the scenery – how did you manage to miss this one basic point?"

"That's not true," the Lady-with-the-Hat protested, "all I did was look out the window, the scenery's lovely."

"And so, Madame, you missed this one basic point," the driver replied, "because you didn't read your travel guide, a person traveling in an unfamiliar country needs to read her travel guide."

"All right," the Lady-with-the-Hat conceded, "but why did she only invite me? Why not invite you as well?"

"A woman is not allowed to invite a man," said the driver, his eyes on the sky, "that wouldn't be proper, it's the man who must invite the woman, but first he must ask her parents' permission – so what do I do – you see how old she is, her parents are long gone now; even a child can see."

"Oh," said the Lady-with-the-Hat, "I didn't really understand, still, at least you could tell her I'm from Greece – no – from Crete."

"What's the point," the driver replied, "I already told her you're English, that'll do."

"But didn't you ask her what road we have to take?" said the Lady-with-the-Hat.

"It would be better if we stopped somewhere else and asked," said the driver, "this woman doesn't know, she's ignorant."

"Ask her, anyway," said the Lady-with-the-Hat, "it's the whole reason we stopped."

"There's no reason to get angry," the driver said.

"I'm not angry," said the Lady-with-the-Hat, "I'm simply asking that you be so kind as to ask the way to Bukhara, which is the whole reason you chose to stop in front of this house in the first place."

The taxi driver sighed again. "All right," he said, "if you insist."

He began to talk with the Woman-of-the-Loom while he stared off at the horizon. A long conversation ensued while he stared at the sky and the woman focused on her loom. Then they both were quiet. A minute passed, maybe two.

The Lady-with-the-Hat stared at the driver, waiting, but he stared at the sky. Then she looked at the Woman-of-the-Loom, who looked up from the rug she was weaving and gave her a broad smile. "Have you figured out what road we have to take?" she asked the driver.

"No," the driver answered, "she told me if you want to stay for lunch, her grandchildren are coming and she's grilling goat sausages, but I told her you can't stay for lunch because we have to go to Bukhara to buy a rug."

"Well, I want to stay," said the Lady-with-the-Hat, "I've changed my mind and want to stay for lunch. Actually, maybe I'll buy that rug she's working on, it's nearly finished, this one, or maybe some other rug she has inside, please, tell her I'd like to buy this rug or some other rug she has inside, and that I do accept her kind offer to stay for lunch."

Another long conversation ensued between the driver and the Woman-of-the-Loom, who didn't look up from the rug she was weaving, while the Lady-with-the-Hat waited patiently. She began to feel tired and, without asking permission, she sat down on a wooden stool beside the brazier. The sun was warm but the wind off the mountains was chilly, her cheeks were on fire and her feet were frozen.

"The woman says she's sorry," the driver finally said, "but she won't sell you the rug, she's never sold rugs and can't sell any rugs she has inside because they're hers, and she's weaving this one for her grandson who's getting married next month, it's her grandson's wedding gift, why on earth should she sell you her grandson's wedding gift, she's not going to sell you a thing, but she would like you to stay for lunch, because today her grandchildren are coming to celebrate her grandson's engagement and they're bringing two musicians with them, and after the meal her grandson will do the traditional dance and we'll form a circle around him, and I can stay and eat, too, because you've invited me, goat sausages with wild herbs are delicious and it will be a wonderful party, her grandson raises animals, he's twenty years old and dances very well, he knows the ancient songs, he's a poet, and he's bringing along two of his cousins, girls who aren't married yet, one's seventeen, the other, nineteen, but they're not from Samarkand."

"Well, I'm sure it will be a lovely celebration," said the Lady-with-the-Hat, "I'm very curious. But I didn't invite you; this lady invited *me*."

"But if you tell her you've invited me because she's invited you, it's like she invited me; this is the custom with people in these parts, your travel guide probably says so, too, but you wouldn't know because you were too busy watching the scenery go by instead of reading your travel guide. Besides, that isn't the problem, the problem…" and the driver grew mysteriously quiet.

"The problem? What problem?" said the Lady-with-the-Hat.

"The problem," said the driver, "is your hat. This will be a traditional dance, it's a ceremonial dance, everyone will be wearing traditional costumes, I could wear the costume worn by the woman's father – it would be rude not to – but you won't have a traditional costume to wear, and you also can't wear that hat you have on, you can't participate in the circle in that sort of hat, and you also can't participate in the ceremony with your hair down; in these parts the traditional ceremonial hat is absolutely necessary, and your hat…your hat, for this ceremony, it just won't do, it's slightly…slightly ridiculous."

"What's so ridiculous about my hat," said the Lady-with-the-Hat, "it keeps the sun off, it's a woven Panama hat, the same color as your plains, with a small flower, a fresh daisy, on the band."

"Oh, of course it's pretty," the driver answered, "but it won't do for the ceremony – the lady can loan you a traditional hat, though, if you follow her inside. But, sorry, where did you buy this hat?"

"In London," said the Lady-with-the-Hat.

For the first time, the driver looked at the Woman-of-the-Loom, and he said to her in English: "London!" And they began to laugh.

The Woman-of-the-Loom had gotten to her feet and was now standing in the doorway, and she waved for the Lady-with-the-Hat to come inside.

When she came out again, the Lady-with-the-Hat had her hat in one hand and a different hat on her head, a very brightly colored cap that came down over her forehead and was decorated with rows of seed pearls. The driver snapped a photo. The Lady-with-the-Hat, her hat in her hand and the Uzbek cap on her head, managed to force a smile just in time.

"Tell her if I can't buy the rug, I'd at least like to buy the hat," said the Lady-with-the-Hat, her hat in her hand and the Uzbek cap on her head.

The driver couldn't help it, he slapped the steering wheel so the horn sounded, then he burst out laughing. "Madame," he said, "you really didn't read the travel guide, you don't know a thing about this country, this woman is ignorant, she's certainly not from Samarkand, she won't sell you anything because she doesn't know the first thing about money, but for this hat of yours, which she finds silly, she'll trade you two hats, do you have someone in Crete who might want a hat?"

"A sister," the lady stammered, "I have a sister." Then leafing quickly through the little Uzbek guide she'd brought along, she whispered in that language: "Sister."

"Hurrah!" the driver shouted, "today you found two hats, now I'm off to eat at the inn in the nearest town, because I wasn't invited here, but I will return for the dance, there'll be some fine liquor."

And he sped off, leaving a cloud of dust behind him.

# A *Curandeiro* in the City
# on the Water

Was it a song? A dream? There was *something* beyond the glass. He opened the windows. It was the sirocco wind, and high above, clouds raced across the sky and gathered on the horizon, a glimmer of silver, the imprint of dawn.

That night he'd dreamt about a Snark. But it was no animal, no zoomorphic or anthropomorphic creature, it was an Everything and a Nothing: it was pure immanence, like some awful presence you couldn't see. You felt it. And he'd definitely "felt" it. And he sensed that only some could feel it, but they couldn't understand it. A phrase came to mind (or was it a poem?): "Great madness is intelligence through the comprehending gaze; great intelligence is the purest form of madness, and in this the Majority prevails, as it does in all the rest." And then he thought: mad as a hatter. But who was mad as a hatter – was it he? No, he felt old, that's all. He studied himself in the mirror: "Uoy t'nod leef dlo, ym dneirf, uoy *era* dlo."

The mirror never answered back, though for over sixty years he'd known this strange creature who seems to be us, but in reverse: the axis of our image in reverse, what's really on the left seems to be on the right, and vice versa. And the mirror's language, what the hell language did it speak? Some dialect from a distant planet?

What's more, it was hot. Desperately hot, and the light was dazzling: an exaggerated light, unnatural, like an overexposed photo. He went to the window. He could barely see out. He held his hand to his forehead like the brim of a hat. Down the street, two people were waiting for the tram, but the metal trapezoid had come off the wires and the conductor was trying to shift it with a long pole. But the man's pole wasn't moving forward or backward; the man was still, like a single frame in a film that's suddenly stopped. And the two people waiting under the platform roof were still as well, with a fixedness that seemed eternal.

He glanced toward the tobacco shop across the street just as someone was coming out, and he had the distinct impression this person already knew he'd be at the window, because his hand was already raised in greeting. That is: the man getting ready to leave the tobacco shop had already prepared this greeting before he himself had gone over to the window. So strange. Ah, but he knew this man, it was Esteves. He also waved, but Esteves didn't move, he stood there, his little hand up, distinctively, definitively raised. He jerked back from the window. What was going on? He considered phoning Ferruccio and went into the living room. He dialed the number and a female voice answered, an artificial voice, the kind made on a synthesizer: "We're sorry, this number is no longer valid, but if you want to leave a message, go right ahead."

Obviously, a wrong number. What a bunch of jokers, he thought, the world's full of idiots. He redialed, paying close attention. The same synthetic voice said: "The person you're looking for has snuck off. If you want to leave a message, you have an eternity at your disposal." He slammed the receiver down. He realized he was soaked with sweat. He hesitated. What the hell was this? He dialed the number again. This time, the voice was hostile: "Geez, don't be such a ball buster! – decide already – you want to leave a message or not?" He hung up. His shirt was soaking. He thought: "No – this can't be." He redialed. "Now, listen, Mister," the same voice said, "even a machine can only take so much: you want to leave this damned message, or don't you?"

"I'll leave a message," he answered automatically, not even considering how absurd this sounded.

"So leave one already," said the answering machine.

"Listen," he said, not sure what to say. "Listen…tell Ferruccio… well, I…yesterday in my mailbox…I found…I found a hand-written letter, and it seemed like a child wrote it, I'm not sure what to say… well…it was upsetting, and I'm not going to rule out the possibility that my nightmare last night was because of this letter – no – I'm almost certain it *was* the letter that caused my nightmare…but…but I want to describe my dream to Ferruccio."

"So what did the letter say?" the voice asked.

"Just a second," he said, "it's in Spanish, it's here on my desk, the first part's all in capital letters, like typeface, like a newspaper headline."

"Read it," said the voice.

"*Testimonio verdadero que nadie quiere creer de la Hermana Consuelo de los Dolores y de todas las Desgracias de este Mundo, que asistió el Papa Luciani al render el alma.*" He paused. "And here there's an asterisk to a footnote."*

"Read the footnote."

He read: "*La Hermana Consuelo fue atropellada en frente de la iglesia del Sagrado Corazón en Roma por un pirata del asfalto que nunca fue atrapado, y murió instantaneamente.*"**

"Logical," the voice said, "now the rest of the letter too."

"*El inclinó dulcemente la cabeza en la almohada, parpedeó como lo hacía Liz Taylor en la película Lassie y dijo: hermana, oye, en el último instante de mi vida esperava ver la imagen luminosa de Nuestra Señora de Pompei o de Fátima, y sin embargo estoy viendo el Snark, no hay duda, hermana, todo es de una esnarquidad absoluta, una especie de embotellamento, el caos primordial, como un Alzhimer infinito... Ustedes están perdidos, hermanita. Y se murió.*"****

---

* "Real evidence which no one wants to believe of Sister Consuelo of Pain and All the Troubles of this World, who attended to Papa Luciani when he rendered his soul to God."

** "Sister Consuelo was struck by a hit-and-run-driver in front of the Chiesa del Sacro Cuore in Rome and died instantly."

*** "He gently lay back on the pillow, batted his eyelashes like Liz Taylor in *Lassie*, and said: 'Listen, Sister, in my last moments, I thought I'd see the shining image of Our Lady of Pompeii or Fátima, but what I'm seeing instead is the Snark, there's no doubt about it, Sister, everything's an absolute snarkness, a sort of gridlock, a primordial chaos, like endless Alzheimer's...you're all toast, dear Sister.' And he died."

"Logical," said the answering machine, "it's all very logical. On the path to Heaven, he'd learned they were handing the world over to the Snark and so they planned... Bam! Understand?"

"Not a damn word," he answered, "but last night I also dreamt about the Snark, and I feel very uneasy. So what is this Snark – do you know?"

"It's what is actually flowing through the veins of History," the voice answered. "Now, how about telling me your dream?"

"Sure," he said, "but please no interrupting, it's hard enough to tell your dreams."

"I promise," the voice said.

He began to tell his dream.

"One thing I do know: I could see them, but they couldn't see me. Something was keeping me out of sight, a wall or screen of some kind, I couldn't quite tell, but it kept me hidden. And yet I also had the distinct feeling that I was exposed, out in the light, like I was in the front row of a theater. And from that front row, I could watch them. Their movements were extremely sharp for me, just like their body odor. A heavy, sickly-sweet odor that I'd smelled once before, long ago, in a morgue in a city in a foreign country, where I'd gone to identify the body of a friend of mine killed by the police. It was a show, this I knew. But it was a show performed in all its naked truth, and it was true because it was truer than true. The scene unfolded on the wharfs in the harbor of a Mediterranean city, and a noonday sun shed a troubling light over the scene, the kind of light sometimes found in flash photos. A steel ship was docked at the pier, obviously a battleship, mysterious and ominous, like an ironclad in an old film. It was fitted with cannons and a tricolor flag flapping in the wind. I felt an overwhelming sense of disquiet. Something foul, I felt, was underway. But I could also tell it was all unreal, all the fruit of my imagination, let loose, as in a dream. I told myself: why do they want me to dream this dream? Who's forcing me to dream? And I told myself: you have to wake up, you mustn't let them force you to dream a dream you don't want to dream, they're worming their way into your soul, they want to overwhelm you. Lounging in my easy chair, watching the pier from my small window, safe from prying eyes, I caught sight of a man's face, his expression triumphant. An oily liquid oozing from his thinning hair was slick on his cheeks, glowing in the artificial sunlight. 'Good evening,' he said in a cloying voice, 'I'm Doctor Melanoma, from next door, my every service is a service to the Services, so this is the name I prefer to go by, for my sarcomatic nature, which is necessary to officiate over the solemn proceedings that will determine the fate of our village! Today, the billy-goat god we humbly serve gathers together his worshipping throng. Let the procession begin!' And there came the first resounding notes of a military anthem. A loud chorus, no, a clamoring accompanied that pompous music. But you couldn't catch all the words. Just a phrase here and there, like the isolated syntagms of a litany: 'War, war, war.' And then other whispered words, lofty, unfinished, mutilated syllables: 'butchered limbs – ah, ah, ah – mangled bodies – ah, ah, ah – crushed heads – ah, ah, ah – blood, blood, blood.' The parade showed at the end of the pier, and advanced. A sinister, frightening character was up front. An obese man with disheveled hair and flushed cheeks. His enormous body ended at the groin and rested on a low wooden platform on four small wheels. This was his means of transport: the fat man steered and maneuvered, pushing off the ground with his hands. Above his makeshift dolly was a banner with the words: *Combatants and veterans of the wars for civilization*. The parade leader dug in his pocket, pulled out a star-covered flag, which he wrapped around his obese stump of a body, and shouted: 'Forward, heroes – for stardust! Long live Trash!' A woman walking behind him screamed like a fury: 'I'm his wife! I'm his wife! Through the truth of television, we taught them Italians how to fuck!' I began to feel frightened. And then behind this man, music rang out: a brass band playing a famous swing tune: *Stardust*. I looked closer. The musicians seemed right out of some horrific Grimms' fairy tale, beggarly and thieving. The trombonist was tall and gangly, and between bursts of horn-blowing, he turned and whispered to the legless man, 'You're the most intelligent of us, so we democrats of the Bollocks are coming with you.' The other musicians, equipped with flutes, clarinets, cornets, and small trumpets, had medals covering their chests and signs hanging around their necks to indicate their high office. Then out of this group stepped a haughty individual in a fine suit who looked around icily. He moved toward the right side of the pier, where a man in a black leather trench coat was watching, a pistol and a roll of dollar bills in his hand. The man in the fine gray suit said, 'I've got the photos identifying all those siding with the enemy,' his voice scornful, 'finally, this country's free to denounce its traitors. Who cares – there are many to cover the lawsuits.' Then he turned in my direction, and for a second I thought he was speaking to me, that he'd seen me, though he was probably addressing the crowd. His voice sounded metallic, and he enunciated his words and used simple syntax. 'If you ever recognize me,' he hissed, 'be careful about saying my name. One of our fine officers might like to pay you a visit at home, you know. He might sprinkle a little white powder around – don't be stupid, my friend – just stick to writing your novels. We'll put up with you, but you behave yourself.' Behind him came other little men in double-breasted jackets. Their expressions were menacing and each man held his hand out, palm up, with words written on it in ink: Ministry of the Bollocks Republic. And only then did I realize that everyone marching in the procession had a prosthetic limb: some had wooden legs, others metal arms, artificial limbs of shining steel that they waved in jubilation. On each one's jacket lapel a small card read, *Veterans of the wars of civilization*, and meanwhile, a cheerful old fellow dressed like an altar boy sprinkled each of them with holy water. And then the fat amputated torso screamed, 'Let the Sabbath begin! God save civilization, the civilization we've forced upon the world for all these years, our civilization, true civilization, what we've devoted our Services to at the cost of others' lives, lives that luckily we could lock up in stadiums in Chile and toss out of planes into the seas of Argentina. Long live the Snark!'

"The music grew more intense, as if caught in a frenzy. The procession of the lame, the wretched survivors of so many battles, those who'd been destitute, impoverished all these years, now finally broke into Saint Vitus's dance, brought on by the panicked euphoria of understanding that they were still alive, that they still had vigorous blood permeating their prosthetic limbs. And the Sabbath turned to torment, a pandemonium of screams, of heaving bodies, and a dog barked furiously from the shadows, but above it all, what passed through my eardrums was the crackling voice of a witch, her face shriveled and lustful, while she shrieked with delight: 'Let's embrace him anyway, let's embrace him anyway!' My nausea was stronger than the dream – I jolted awake. It was the middle of the night, with only electric snow showing on the television screen from stations off the air."

There wasn't a sound on the other end. He wondered if they were still connected. "Can you hear me?" he asked.

"I hear you," the voice said, "you're suffering, just like your friend Ferruccio. You need a *curandeiro*, too, your friend went looking for one, but good *curandeiros* are hard to come by, extremely hard to come by, anyway, you're a lucky man, in this city of yours, there just happens to be a fantastic *curandeiro* who can absorb all of your disquiet, I know everything, trust me."

"But who are you?"

"Listen," the voice said, sounding friendly, "I have many names, today my name's Unconscious, though I'm quite conscious, you hear? The Ancients called me Pythia, but you can call me Pizzi-Pazio, that'll do."

"Pizzi-Pazio?" he repeated.

"Yes, a *petit-nom* for my friends, but that's just between us."

"Don't worry, Madam Pizzi-Pazio," he said, "but how do I find my *curandeiro*?"

"I'll guide you from here, from my Anywhere Out of the World," the voice said. "All you have to do is follow the poem."

"I don't understand," he said.

"Try a little harder," the voice said. "You always loved that poem, don't you remember? *Cette ville est au bord de l'eau; on dit qu'elle est bâtie en marbre... voilà un paysage selon ton goût, un paysage fait avec la lumière et le minéral, et le liquide pour les réfléchir...* Now then, you start walking beside those ancient buildings, under the vaults that once held the colonial markets, the clamor brought with the tall ships, the gloom after they parted… Walk along the river, toward its mouth, you'll see, it won't be hard, you'll arrive at a modern-day temple where the surviving muses have taken refuge. You have to go in, look around, enjoy what you find, because it's something that someone's broken his back over for you to enjoy. And with this, I bid you farewell, do take care of yourself."

Silence followed and then the voice, no longer friendly, now monotone, said: "To end the recording press the pound key and hang up."

He hung up and went outside. It was noon, and the sun was blinding.

*Ariettas*

# The Arrival of
# Doctor Pereira

Yesterday morning Doctor Pereira returned to pay me a visit. He came by mail from Italy, arriving on this Lisbon street. Unaware, I opened the large yellow envelope, which seemed to contain a pasteboard, and I surprised him while he sat at a small table in the Orquídea café having a lemonade. He, too, looked at me, surprised that I was looking at him. He'd loosened his tie, his jacket hung over his chair – the *Lisboa* poking out from the pocket; he held a teaspoon in midair, as though, in realizing I was watching him, he'd stopped stirring his lemonade. He looked at me over his small round glasses  similar to mine, his eyebrows raised, questioning, like someone who might ask, "So what're *you* looking at?" I almost wanted to answer, "Look, you're the one who's called on *me* – read what's there below your portrait: *To Tabucchi from Dr. Pereira*"; but

I didn't, because I already knew what he'd say. And the usual skirmish would begin.

"Actually, you're the one who called on *me*!"

"No, no, what are you saying – you called on me first!"

It was always this way with Pereira: before writing him and while writing him, especially at night, before going to sleep, my eyelids lowering and my internal voices feeling soothed.

But it was different now, this was no longer an evocation, a subtle game to make him appear, to call him or be called by him, to talk, so he'd talk about himself, so he'd declare to me what he wanted to declare. From *formerly invoked*, meaning, from bringing him forth with my voice, he'd passed to *mutually invoked*. Someone had mutually invoked his ghost, which materialized in a picture. And now the icon of Pereira was there before me, solid, visible in all its "pereirity." And this convocation was the work of the medium Giancarlo Vitali.

"For now, let's set you over here, Doctor Pereira," I told him and added, "tomorrow I'll find a better spot, then we'll have time to pick up where we left off with our mutual diatribe. Thank you though for coming to my home, I always came to your home and never invited you here."

Lisbon, October 1997

# The Fixed Traveler

Clutching a steamship to his chest like a child clutches a toy, the Fernando Pessoa of António Costa Pinheiro is traveling while sitting at a table. In the glasses resting on his nose, two seagulls soar; the other glasses lying on the table show reflections of other steamships, evocations of other trips and other distant seas.

The most important, the one true trip of his life, Pessoa made at seventeen, from Durban, where he grew up, and returning to Lisbon, the city he would never leave again. He'd parted for Durban when he was seven, with his young, widowed mother who was joining her second husband, married by proxy, in the British colony where he served as Portuguese consul. At thirteen, Fernando returned to Lisbon for a while with his new family (his parents, sister, and younger brother) and also traveled to the Azores. But his real *nostos* was his definitive return to his home country. This was both a life-choice (his siblings chose an English university instead) and a pathway, as he boarded the transatlantic steamer, the Herzog, which sailed to Lisbon along the east coast of Africa.

That memorable steamer voyage, from the Indian Ocean to the Red Sea through the Suez Canal to the Mediterranean to the Atlantic and finally to his birth city, is a voyage described in Álvaro de Campos's long, early work, *Opiário*. A kind of long, symbolist-Parnassian poem, heavy with irony, a seeming parody of the decadent movement. On-board gala parties, smoking-rooms, flashy moons over the Suez Canal, opium and morphine, those "crazy years" and their frivolity, hiding the tragic grimace – à la Fitzgerald – of that world. And especially, an ineptitude toward life ("To feel life languish and weaken"), the same ineptitude that could be said of Baudelaire, Proust, Benjamin, Beckett ("Bon qu'à ça, it's the only thing I'm good at," Beckett answered when they asked him why he wrote).

But it was all a game. And in this painting, "little" Fernando holds his play-toy tight to his chest. There would be other travels: heroic, visionary, furious travels full of adventures and discoveries, but all of these, imaginary. And most of all, the travels of others, of the Portuguese sailors described in the *Triumphal Ode*, in the *Maritime Ode*, in *Message*. And then dream travels to far-off islands that were also ironically false, flashy, trimmed with palm trees, pink and blue, like colored copperplate engravings.

The great traveler of travels never taken ("The vigil of never parting / at least without vigils to keep"), the man who played with life like it was a dream and with the dream like it was life; that man is here, in this portrait by António Costa Pinheiro, in all the solemnity of his game. Pessoa was extremely reluctant, and ultimately managed to avoid having an identity card, especially one with his own photo, what he called the "provisional visible representation" of himself.

If he were to come back to life, he'd probably take his ironic revenge on what we view as objectivity by transforming this painting into a photo that he'd put on his "Traveler of the Infinite" ID card.

# Like a Mirror

Between Valerio Adami's dream ghosts turned into the geometry of reality or Camilla Adami's geometry of reality turned into figures in the world of dreams, who are we to believe?

Who is truer, Freud or Euclid? Who is truer, Hypnos or the primate, through the reversed binoculars of our primitive innocence, that stares back at us in puzzlement? Hypnos, Onirós, Pythagoras, Euclid, Darwin: dream/reality. We think we know everything, and we know so little.

Considering the binary universe to which Nature compels us, considering the "sense" of something that relentlessly exists in reality or that the dream relentlessly imposes on us, art has always found a "different" sense. We can know the reality existing around us, but it will remain separate. Even the dreams we believe to be ours, are not. We're not the ones dreaming: the *dream* wants to be dreamed and so, to exist, it uses us.

Are we reality or semblance? Baroque artists loved this dilemma, making it the linchpin to their art. And out of this dilemma (to be or not to be; or if life is a dream) came modern art, which our period has loaded with new meanings, with new questions and other nagging thoughts, and yet the dilemma is still fundamentally the same: the comparison between what is tangible and measurable (according to Euclid) and what pertains to nonbeing. Because according to the Ancients, Hypnos (the son of Night and Erebus and Thanatos's twin) belongs to the dimension of nonbeing or the state of being. Our lives run on this binary track, yet there's something higher that guides our journey, even when it comes to biology: Chance (Chance and Necessity, Jacques Monod would have said). Art belongs to this category: it marries Chance and Necessity; it creates a balance between the illusoriness of the dream and the evidence of reality. It produces a "third state."

While I look at the works of Camilla and Valerio, one in front of the other, I'm struck by the idea that they really do function like a mirror: what's right of the axis reflects what's to the left, and vice versa, the image returns inverted, it's the same but isn't, it says the same thing yet doesn't. Or it says two different things while they are the same. It's a "returned gaze," as Taoist philosophers refer to the mirror.

These figures of Camilla and Valerio Adami are solemn, at times severe, often in distress or pain. And yet they also seem to project a strange smile. An unseen smile. Perhaps to see it, you need to move to a privileged point in space, an ideal distance from the two mirrors looking at each other. At that hypothetical point, which is a geometric place, you can see the smile not there on both faces. A smile that doesn't exist in realty but that the mind perceives, and it too belongs to the order of geometric places. It's that *sub-risu* of Leonardo's mysterious figures, like the

Archaic Greek statues Ortega y Gasset explored in his wonderful 1909 text. That invisible smile we still perceive, what Walter Pater defined as *unfathomable*.

Lewis Carroll applied the geometric place to the Cheshire Cat that subtracted its body from reality, leaving behind only its smile. I believe that right here, in this geometric place pertaining only to aesthetic emotion, the spirits of the respective figures leave their ghost behind on the canvas, and then they meet. And like an arc of electric current, they smile at having found each other.

# Portraits of Stevenson

It's amazing to see how well art can travel, as Jankélévitch defines this (the language of one art that "travels" toward the language of another). The French philosopher's proposition concerns the pairing of music and literature but certainly applies to all the arts. It's more than a simple homage and is also different from the "borrowing" that postmodern theorists love so well. It's a chosen affinity, a tribal recognition, derived from the father, yet completely different, as the new individual with his own basic physiognomy must be. It is, as Borges said, the chronological labyrinth of art that blows diachrony apart: "the Before and the After," if memory serves, "that merit the same law."

I'm indulging in these somewhat abstruse musings while leafing through Tullio Pericoli's graphic work, in Dante Albieri Editore's wonderful portfolio (*Morgana 2*): a series of plates referring partly to Robinsonesque seascapes and mainly to Robert Louis Stevenson and his narrative world.

Stevenson, I believe, was oxygen for all those who fell in love with him as teenagers – a time that many found to be suffocating. Of course the form of suffocation varied from teenager to teenager. Let's say: someone's stuck in bed with a knee fracture, maybe in the 1950s in Italy. And the Polesine Flood occurs, or some similar disaster, and everyone has to help, and the Ladies' Aid Society (someone must remember this charitable organization) is collecting old clothes to send to the poor flood victims, and meanwhile someone's singing "Old Boot," or some similar song, because the Sanremo Festival's playing on the radio, and meanwhile this boy, this invalid, has to read *Heart* or even worse, the abridged version of *The Betrothed*. Things like that, practically universal, in the sense that everyone in their own way, in every country on earth, will have their Polesine Floods and their Aid Societies, and will have to endure – in other forms and other languages, of course – their Old Boots and their *Hearts* and their abridged versions of *The Betrothed*.

And this boy, this poor, temporary invalid, is suffocating even if he doesn't know it. Until someone (an uncle, who will become a figure of salvation for him) brings him a Stevenson novel, *Treasure Island*, say. And like a miracle, the suffocating boy begins to breathe. Because there's suddenly oxygen: wind filling the sails of a ship as it glides toward some remote island, not a literal island but the quintessential island, that island hidden inside us all that means someplace else, the place of our desires, the where we hope exists, the something different from here.

The island of Utopia? The fantastic, palm-dotted, south-sea islands that eased the consumption and melancholy of the Crepuscular poets? The come-away-with-me of a beautiful song he would listen to when he was older? All this and many other things as well, everything that enters the space of the imaginary journey. And Stevenson knew better than anyone how to sail toward the mythic geography of the spirit.

He had his reasons: he was born and raised in Edinburgh, a city of fog and granite. With his unhealthy lungs, he spent his adolescence in the hospital, slipping out of bed to open the windows: his body and spirit needed oxygen. And he found it. He went on real journeys, crossed entire countries riding on a donkey's back, boarded steamers bound for the emigrants' Americas. But most of all, he crossed over time and space, let the sails of his imagination fill with wind. Then, for his last years, he chose a real South Sea Island, and for his final resting place, the top of a volcano, where his native friends carried him on a litter, so he could stay up there, breathing better forever.

And so I leaf through Tullio Pericoli's Stevenson portfolio. The suffocating heat lifts, is gone with the wind. The vigor filling these sails, filling these stories of consumption in Edinburgh, swirls all around these drawings: in the landscapes stretching out to the horizon, in the depths of the ocean superimposed over the floor, in the flowing hair of the writer, his back to us, in his writer-sailor jacket, in the carpet he tramples, map of the possible, in the clouds and waves. Here is the freedom to stay in the world, to think, imagine, write. And here, too, is the freedom to draw. With no critical, no interpretive – no structural – demands; the one suffocating takes in oxygen, and listens to the wind of these drawings.

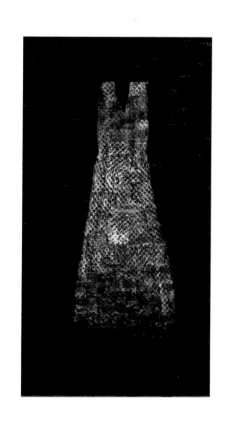

# Spices, Lace, Distant Journeys

Dear Piero Pizzi Cannella,

If we were to follow the Ancients' belief in the *nomen omen*, I'd almost have to begin this letter half-jokingly (but only seemingly) by suggesting that while these paintings of yours (icons emerging from the background like plankton rises in distant night seas, shining in the light of the Southern Cross) were certainly guided by your hand, they were also guided by the name of the wielder of that hand – your name – meaning lace and cinnamon, and that such a name is tied to that mysterious law that the Ancients believed was guided by the arcane power of the word.

And so, continuing down this path, perhaps it's not too outlandish to suspect that the lace in your paintings is one code of that unsolvable rebus that "explains" without being explained, and that is the language of art. And in your case, I must admit, is also a formalized game: one which, from the Ancients on (I can't stress the Ancients enough), has been symbolized many times over, perhaps under the delusion that geometric forms, with their perimeters and angles, can circumscribe dreams and desires. And here I might slip into a dangerous labyrinth myself were I to begin speaking of the labyrinth, composed of coordinate axes, nodes, intersections and boxes, which, to the Cretans meant the objective of the tested hero; to the Asians, the search for balance; and in Romanesque cathedrals, the substitute path to Jerusalem for stay-at-home pilgrims. And it would be riskier still to evoke the four stylized universal elements on certain mosaic arrow crosses, the geometric arrangements of the Megalithic menhirs, the diamond pattern of the Mayan pyramids, and so on, up to crossword puzzles or the various brainteasers that even the most recent literature relies on, look at the late Georges Perec and his friends in Oulipo.

But if "everything is symbol and analogy," as a poet wrote who experienced the alluring mystery hidden below the skin of the real, then what might the snakeskin of your works, and all those curious scales, be hiding? A snake, I'd say, that's less a python than a pythoness, considering the almost sacerdotal cut to the icons, their Sybils' copes swallowed up by time, all theodicy lost (if they ever had it), but not their rightful sanctity. Who exactly were these women, and who can say where they lived, or when? Not so much that they're providing us with answers, but making us question. If this was their function, I believe you bring it back, as the artist knows how to, by saying in new ways the most ancient of things (I seem to be dwelling on the Ancients, sorry to obsess). And the question that they posed and that you make your own by taking over their sign language, giving it new meaning, echoes implicitly in this city where your works are displayed. Actually, I'd say this is just the right place, this ancient city's not a bad location at all, loaded with symbols, images, icons that may no longer hold the meaning they once held, but are still just as vibrant. A city filled with allegorical figurines, obscure and enigmatic figurines, with a bestiary of fantastic creatures that might just be fantastic forever, like certain Medieval tapestries telling their timeless, placeless stories.

But perhaps, dear Pizzi Cannella, it's time to add my *in conclusion* to this slightly crazy letter. It's gotten out of hand: I haven't just let my imagination go, I've lost myself in reveries. I'll try to refocus this wandering letter that's carried me off to Cretan palaces and Medieval cathedrals, and so now with your permission, I'll turn to India. Like you said yourself, the ghosts of these paintings (female ghosts, in my opinion) were made with the old Indian block prints once used for printing women's saris, and who knows, perhaps are still used in certain remote parts of India. Designs and woven patterns that on the canvasses of this clothing had their own meaning, and on your canvasses, have another: not just because you give them new meaning, but because function creates form. And therefore, taking advantage of the fact that logic is logic – as long as it functions inside a system (even if in itself it would seem illogical), sticking to the subject I started with, I'd like to end with the second part of your name. Because, if this lace (pizzi) comes from India, what better spice than cinnamon (cannella)? The Romans were already familiar with cinnamon, which they called "cassia" and even used to scent their wine. And the Venetians who traded in the lands of Indus were particularly clever at getting Europeans to value cinnamon. But it was the Portuguese who were the most tied to the spice, making it part of their pharmacopeia, and reeking of it slightly (like a woman's ghost lingers in our memory more than in our bed – or perhaps we might say here, "in our imagination"); it was the Portuguese – my dear friends, as you know – who, in the middle of our now ending millennium (thanks to their explorer Vasco da Gama), rounded the Cape of Storms, renamed it the Cape of Good Hope, arrived in Calicut, and sailed up the coast of India, to Goa, where they established a Portuguese viceroyalty, and brought a bit of the West to the East. And in turn, a bit of the East to us.

Indeed, in that distant sixteenth century, Europe truly began to change, because it discovered the world was round. Or better – it stepped out of the Medieval Period and into the Renaissance, as my elementary school teacher, in her wisdom, liked to tell us. And there was another, too, who, in his way, brought the East to Europe: the botanist Garcia da Horta (here, too, a strong nomen-omen, as this name means "Garcia of the Garden"). He was a humanist, a Portuguese scientist, a Jew, who may have gone to India because the Inquisition, extremely active then in Portugal, gave him no rest. And there, in Goa, in 1563, he published an extraordinary book, *Colóquio dos Simples e drogas da* Índia (*A Discussion of the Herbs and Spices of India*), which was simultaneously a book of medicine, pharmacology, and natural philosophy. And which was quite famous back then, because it was translated into Latin and many other languages (including Italian) and published in the great cultural centers of Europe, like Antwerp and Paris.

Dear Pizzi Cannella, sometimes, when an interviewer asks what great man from the past I'd like to meet, I think about Garcia da Horta. Because I'm certain that this Portuguese Jew, who was one of the great botanists of his time; who patiently, humbly classified and studied the medicinal plants of India; who appreciated and tested their virtues; who was a friend of Camões; who disappeared into nothing; and who was tried posthumously, his bones then burned by order of the Court of the Holy Office of Goa (fanaticism has a long tradition); I'm certain, as I was saying, that this gentleman, Mr. Garcia da Horta, and I would get along nicely.

Looking at a painting can carry you away. And rightly so – this is the real beauty of art – it lets us steer where we see fit. And if this voyage seems like a game to some, it might not to you, Pizzi Cannella, because you know better than I how much art is done "for kicks," as a game. But a serious game. Because if art is something of a game, it's also something that keeps us from dying.

Your admirer,
Antonio Tabucchi

# Dear Wall, I'm Writing You…

"Dear Milena, sorry to be answering your postcard a month late, but I haven't been feeling well, now I'm a little better. How are you? Dear Milena! I knew another girl in Rome named Milena, but she's dead . . ."

Once upon a time there was . . . Kafka! That might seem like what comes next. No, dear readers, once upon a time there was a patient in a mental hospital. I may have begun this short letter with Milena, illness, and a macabre sense of irony, but that's a trick—this isn't about Kafka. It's about someone who could have been a main character in a Kafka story, and his name is NOF4 (the acronym of his signature), that is, Nanetti Oreste Fernando. NOF4 (Nannetti) is the author of a provocative book, and like all books, this one is composed of thousands of words. But not on paper—this book is graffiti on over a hundred meters of wall.

Under the initiative of the Local Health Authority (the laudable USL n. 15 in Volterra, to be exact), this "book" has become a regular paper book published by Pacini di Pisa as a supplement to the journal

*Neopsichiatria* and edited by Professor Carmello Pellicanò. I learned about Nannetti's work a couple of years ago, through my friend Amedeo Cappelli, a linguist in that workshop for "creative scientists" that is the Institute for Computational Linguistics in Pisa. I'd always intended to go and see Nannetti's work for myself, yet never found the time. But now that I'm actually holding his writing in my hands – holding his paper book – I have no choice but to go to Volterra to see his real "stone book": what Nannetti Oreste Fernando, during his eleven years in an insane asylum, wrote on the wall that imprisoned him.

Fernando Nannetti's story is as follows. He was born in Rome in 1927, his father unknown. In 1934, he was taken in by a charitable institution. In 1937, he entered an institute for the mentally handicapped and was then removed because he was suffering from a bone disease and so was admitted to the Forlanini Hospital in Rome. Afterwards, some incident occurred that I know nothing about, and he was accused of resisting arrest and had to undergo psychiatric evaluation. He was found "completely mentally incompetent" and acquitted of the charge, and wound up in a forensic psychiatric hospital, in the judicial section of the hospital in Volterra. In 1961, he was transferred to the civilian section of this same hospital. In 1972, he was discharged, and with his pension from the Municipality of Rome, he was taken in by the Bianchi Institute of Volterra, where he lives today.

For eleven years, from 1961 to 1972, NOF4 wore down belt buckle after belt buckle of his in-patient uniforms, scratching on the asylum wall, carving out a mysterious story (that narratologists would define as "plotless"), interspersed with human figures and geometric designs. A message along one hundred and eighty meters of wall, fifty-three meters of it still remaining today, about one hundred twenty centimeters off the ground. This is NOF4's book.

But what is this "book," and what story does it tell? I ask myself this, because NOF4's book obviously has narrative intent: it clearly wants to tell something. Above all, it speaks of Nannetti's private odyssey and his journey toward Ithaca (which is explicitly mentioned). It speaks of his family, in a sort of recurring motif. A family consisting of a fairly somatic-looking tribe of characters (the people of this clan are all "tall, dark, spinachy, with a Y nose") who look nothing like Nannetti's blood relatives, whom he never met (in all those years, no one ever visited Fernando Nannetti). They are, let's call them, his "somatic brothers of choice," and seem to be Pius XIII, one Alberto the Armored Monkey, and Amadeus of Savoy. And then his book speaks of his father, through the precept, "remember to honor your father." A father Nannetti never met. But the book is also a sort of world vision: there's the memory of Genesis ("Adam and Noah and his ark...Eve and the apple tree and the viper"); a cosmography; a fantastic description of the heavens, of the stars and planets; bits of autobiography. And there's the horror of war ("the spiked path advances over Europe with no territorial conflicts"); and imaginary executions; mysterious deaths; grieving over death; dream journeys; a sort of calendar or scansion of chronological time. A book that contains, through the distortion of madness, what many books contain that treat the story of humanity: cosmogonies, wars, mysteries, pain, joy, piety, fear, love, and death.

I realize a case like Nannetti's warrants psychological study. Yet the USL 115 of Volterra hasn't privileged the issue of psychiatry-writing or confined this work to the world of medicine; instead, they left it up to artists to consider Nannetti's writing: the Volterran sculptor, Mino Trafeli (Nannetti's book is also sculpture); his assistant Aldo Trafeli, who patiently deciphered and transcribed some fragments of the book; and Giuliano Scabia, who wrote the wonderful preface entitled, *The Book of Life*. The original, skillful photographs are the work of Pier Nello Manoni.

And what does it mean that the doctors themselves have been silent about Nannetti's book? I suppose, with this discreet gesture, that the USL psychiatrists had something essential to say: that if mental illness is a mystery, so is writing; and in a work like this, perhaps what predominates isn't so much the mystery of madness as the mystery of writing.

Mino Trafeli, in his commentary on the book flap, traces Nannetti's writing to the idea of poetic expression: "The connection NOF4 has established to his unconscious makes us reflect on what poetry is, on what can be done with knowledge, with a little knowledge, or with a little unhinged knowledge." This "unhinged knowledge" must have greatly impressed Jean Dubuffet, because shortly before he died, he wrote Trafeli to express his admiration for Fernando Nannetti's "extraordinaires inscriptions." Likewise, Michel Thévoz, the curator of the Swiss Musée de l'Art Brut, commented about Nannetti's work that he'd "never seen anything like it."

In his preface, Giuliano Scabia poses questions that I wish to include here: "What is writing? Is it a conversation with the body of the mother, as Barthes suggested? Or an attempt to rule the inner world. Or to stop time. Or to give imprecision to the imprecise. Or a way to hide a secret. Or reveal one. Or a form of melancholy. Or an instrument of power. Or a sketch of impotence. Or a sign in which to entrust the hope of immortality. Or a concrete fragment of the need for memory, memoir. Or a precious relic of civilization. Or a sacred act. Or the technology of the intent mind, like a line of ants walking toward a known and unknown forward. Through writing, historical religions have realized their gods. Through deciphering writing, we've gathered our greatest understanding of extinct civilizations. Writing is increasingly the greatest ballast flowing into electronic memories. And with this reflective writing tapped out on a keyboard, we start to answer our own questions. And what of Nannetti's mural book?"

With this last question, my journey of acknowledgment must stop, outside the San Gerolamo mental hospital that now stands empty. These last years in Volterra, every morning, Nannetti, a semi-free man, has returned to a balustrade of this building to continue his work on the surface of the wall: his writing, twenty-two centimeters wide and a hundred and six meters long. The end of his story, still undeciphered. Covered in brambles and weeds, this last story on the wall of the empty asylum remains, to bear witness.

# Diary of Crete,
# With Hues of Sinopia

*I'm here, lurking around the threshold . . .*
—Giacomo Leopardi

*Knossos, June 1, 2000*

Dear Valerio, I think this might be the best possible place to talk about your painting. I've brought along a bit of your "workshop": your paintings and "teachings," and some photocopies of drawings. And then some readings about Minoan sites, old works I picked up in bookstalls in Florence and Paris, a charming biography of Sir Arthur Evans, for instance, with old pictures of that archaeologist pioneer looking over various works from the palace, what he's just found: he's bent over some rocks jutting out of the ground, and close by, in some clods of dirt, is a Knossos amphora; Sir Arthur looks like a bloodhound that's sniffed out a scent while he studies this unexpected low wall that seems to have sprung up by magic; perhaps he's already picturing it according to some intuited geometry. Yes, clearly, he's understood and grabbed hold of the thread: he thinks he's master of the labyrinth.

Now I'm here, too, sitting on these thousand-year-old stones, it's almost dusk, the few tourists have gone off to eat at the nearby taverns, the chatty, extremely informed guide I took on has exhausted her honorable subject, and from the top of the central staircase, I now sit contemplating the outline of the palace, the stones marking the courtyards, the stables, the animal enclosures, the quarters for the servants, the handmaids, the priests, the rooms for the king and queen, the spaces for all those who lived in this enormous city-dwelling before the great wave raised by an earthquake swept it all away. I look at the labyrinth and I'm reminded of a line from your notes: "The myth is a basic outline of our culture, with knowledge defined by the idea of metamorphosis." I couldn't help but think about the outline in your drawings, to their point of entry, which is unlimited. And I also thought that in a way, with a technique that has truly grown tiresome in our era, your outlined drawings could be defined as open works. The cliché repeated ad nauseam has been turned inside out in an unsettling manner. For if the outline of your works is open to any random entry, then we risk being caught inside, like birds caught in a snare. In this universe we've happily entered, with a freedom bordering on recklessness, we linger, delay our exit, and so are shipwrecked. A shipwreck we've chosen for ourselves, that's seduced us, yet that we refuse to abandon, like Ulysses' sailors who refused all precautionary measures. After all, why tie yourself to the mainmast, why stuff your ears with wax? To return to Ithaca, only to be disappointed and so set sail for other dreams? We might as well get lost where we are, just as we sometimes try to linger in our dreams to put off waking. Virginia Woolf said life is a dream, 'tis the waking that kills us.

Might as well keep dreaming the dream we're offered.


*Knossos, June 2*

There are various methods for prolonging dreams. The Greeks already had some ideas for this, which they learned from the Persians. The dream always begins in the East and sets in the West, dispersed by dawn. Pessoa understood this, and longed for that excessive East he'd never see: the East that everything comes from, faith and the day; the East, magnificent, fanatical, and ardent; the East that is everything we lack, everything we aren't; the East where, maybe, just maybe, Christ still lives. With this concept of the East, Sostratos argued (counter to Iolaus, who upheld an older tradition that the Dream, enveloped by the River of Forgetfulness, resides in Hypnos's cave, and has Death for a sister) that the dream is life, for not only is it credible, it's especially true when it concerns visions of emotions, like an artist's visions, that are always true even when they seem to be imagined. And perhaps this is the meaning of Nietzsche's obscure comment that we need more chaos within ourselves to give birth to a dancing star. Strengthening the dream, then. And it doesn't matter if Sancho Panza makes fun of Don Quixote for his descent into the cave of Montesinos: that extended dream, lasting only a minute, is one of the truest in the West: it carries through an entire novel, an entire literature. It's a mental aerolite, the individual cosmogony Artaud speaks of, that prolonged his dreams in the land of the Tarahumara. A miserable miracle, the other added. But that doesn't matter, maybe Virginia got it wrong, maybe she inverted her terms and didn't realize, when she left her hat floating on the river.


## Knossos, June 3

I stayed overnight somewhere I know you'd like, since you define your-self as "a mountain painter." Along the road inland, after the archaeo-logical site, there's a narrow ravine where even the midday sun doesn't penetrate; a stone double-arch bridge crosses over this ravine, and below is a very clean river where clear, emerald-green pools form with tufts of grass wriggling in the current like women's hair, like Medusa's hair. In this empty, wild place that some writers, poised between aestheticism and mysticism, might define as "panic-inducing," I stripped naked and went for a swim. These situations are risky, we know this just like the man in one of your paintings knows this, as he stares at a pink-fleshed, blushing young faun: they wait in ambush, memories of adolescence, of tall grass, a girl spied from the bushes, a delayed erection, the sense of ridicule, and with it an indefinable shadow of death. I let all these sensations wash over me, while I splashed among the mossy stones, then I put my clothes back on, got in my car, and drove up a steep mountain road and stopped at a simple inn with simple, dusty rooms: rooms with tile floors, over the portico; the bed in my room had a headboard painted with folk motifs and there was a wrought-iron washbasin. In this sort of room, dreams are sterile. Mine certainly was. One of those tired dreams, like a jacket worn your entire life, a dream you have in a room you recognize. Ah, this room – so familiar! On the right, or maybe facing you, there's a mirrored wardrobe. And by the window, there's the bed that saw so much love-making. And by the bed, a window. Strange, you're in the mountains, but that window looks out over the sea, you left it wide open, some nights you'd lean out that window, thinking of far-off voices, listening to the surf, your cigarette glowing in the dark, and then there she was, lightly, behind you, whispering: why don't you come to bed? We were two kids, seeing it now.

The photocopy I brought along of one of your drawings went on the bench that served as a nightstand. It's *The Child's Time to Sleep*, the woman curled up sleeping on a chair while Death in a brigand hat drags a small boy off toward a hill marked with a single cypress. I read that your inspiration for this work was a Holbein woodcut you saw in Basel along with a commentary which ties sleep to death as her little sister. This is Iolaus' view, if slightly less elevated, because in a dream, death's rank is reduced, its noble charter taken away. Which suits the photocopy I brought along: Sister Death, you mustn't think you're so special, our meager dreams are just bad copies of your image. So that night, she must have been frightened and full of pity (which happens to Death sometimes), and in my dream she led that child back by the hand, up to the woman sleeping on the chair, but this woman was no longer the boy's mother, and he was no longer a child, she was lying on a bed by a window overlooking the sea, and she was whispering to him: darling, why don't you come to bed?

And just then I awoke and went to open the shutters, and below I saw a vast olive grove spreading over the entire valley, to Knossos, and I saw that grove rising up as well, on the flanks of the mountain that seemed like the flanks of the woman in my dream.

### Knossos, June 4

Who knows if Sinope still exists, or what its name might be. From that mythical city on the Black Sea like Tomis (though Tomis continued to exist because Ovid died there), the ancients extracted the brown ochre they used to outline in their drawings. While the Cretans used clay ochre for the outlines of their frescoes in Knossos and Phaistos. Perimeters traced with dirt. The colors only added later, perhaps with the unspoken intention of making the perimeters rise up off the ground, as if they might fly.

### Chania, June 6

In the old Venetian-style port of this city once called Canea, I stopped for a drink yesterday at a modest-looking tavern. Tourists aren't comfortable coming here. The drinks are strong, and two men play traditional music on the *lýra*, *rizítika* mainly, but also a Markópoulos from time to time, and these are livelier than tedious *rizítika*, which wear on you, like a sirocco wind. I sat down at a table, and they brought me a glass of wine that was supposed to be white but looked pink. An old man had stopped playing his instrument and now leaning against the door, he raised his glass to me. I raised mine as well. Your catalogue, *Adami's Workshop*, was lying on the table. He seemed curious, and I invited him over, to come and sit.

We began to talk, essentially through hand gestures and those uncommon words someone like me might learn, a few Greek expressions from a travel guide. I'll try to make our conversation intelligible:

"Who's this book?"

"An Italian painter."

"A friend of yours?"

"Yes."

"I too am painter, my name is Manolis." (I get the sense that everyone in Crete is named Manolis.)

"And what do you paint?"

"With lime."

"With lime what?"

"Everything. Houses and everything."

"Only lime?"

"No. Also blue."

"Only lime and blue?"

"There are lots of blues, not just one blue."

And then he said something I didn't understand, so I asked him to write it down for me. I'm not sure, but I think it was something like: "Things are born ugly, that's why they need to be painted." Then he carefully picked up your book and started leafing through it. He stopped on Daphne, and studied her a while. That's Daphne, I said, do you recognize her? Manolis looked at me, his expression authoritative, superior. *Syzygos*, he said, thumping his chest with his finger. And he added the verb, "to paint," in the remote past tense. I didn't understand this word and looked it up in the dictionary at my hotel. *Syzygos* meant "wife." His meaning eludes me. Had Manolis perhaps painted his wife, this man who painted houses white and blue? What did he mean? Had he painted her portrait?

*Sfakiá, June 9*

I'd like some paper, I told the boy working at the tavern, I need to write. In Greek, the word, *Chriázome* (to need) has a connotation slightly different from our verb, because this word doesn't indicate need in the strictest sense, but something vaguely mysterious, its nature hidden. Something is needed, but what isn't particularly clear.

The name of this tavern is Minos, and the boy is of course Manolis. Looking apologetic, he brought me a yellow notepad, the kind for writing up restaurant checks, and this is what I'm currently writing on, with the page rubber-stamped: "Minos Tavern. Original Greek Food." Having a "need" like mine, one referring to something internal, to a sort of mental representation within, urging you on, that you see or hear in an entirely autistic way – for this is all you see or hear – this "need" reminds me of a Cavafy poem, where the only voices are internal voices speaking only to the one who hears them, who is at once broadcaster and receiver. What a magnificent, vicious circle, that of the *acusmatón*, as defined by the Fathers of the Church. Today we're left with that weak diagnosis of a "sound hallucination," as it's termed in psychiatric manuals, or even worse, "auricular disturbances," from the dictionary. In short: either neurological or otolaryngologist.

I remember one afternoon, at your home in Paris, you told me that you searched for a color for your images like you would a sound, because for you color has the same composition as musical notes. I underlined something you'd written down: "How to capture the hiss of the wind in a fireplace? The color, phoneme of the image." Rimbaud colored vowels like they were fingerprints. "The quantity of words is limited, that of accents is infinite," Diderot remarked in the *Salon of 1767*. Diderot, philosopher and author of *Letter on the Deaf and Dumb for the Use of Those Who Hear and Speak,* goes on to say: "Intonation is the very image of the soul rendered with inflections of the voice." And such an intonation, he continues, *est come l'arc-en-ciel*, is like the rainbow.

The human voice is a rainbow: an imperceptible gradation, green already turned to violet, to yellow, to orange. Anger, tenderness, agony, melancholy, seduction, irony: human emotions expressed through intonations of the voice, what Diderot compares to colors of the rainbow.


*Chania, June 10*

Dear Valerio, tomorrow I'll be leaving this island. The photocopies of your works I left for Manolis, as promised, in the tavern where they play the *pendozális*. Fill the squares with a different color, a childhood coloring book of mine suggested, and something strange will appear. Perhaps these past few days, this is what I've done. Manolis will fill in the squares in his own way, maybe with white and blue. We paint the way we can.

A few months ago, I was chatting with one of my son's former classmates, who's actually now an astrophysicist working in the Paris CNR. Considering the source, I asked him for the latest news on discoveries in experimental physics, meaning, the latest news on the Universe. And in a very straightforward manner, he told me the Universe was finished. I asked him, cautiously, in what sense. In the sense that it's been determined by now that the Universe is a mass of expanding energy, he answered very calmly, and so it's finished. And where would you say it's expanding to? I asked. Into nothing, he answered, as if this were the most normal thing in the world. And what is nothing? I asked, foolishly. Simple, the scientist answered, completely at ease, nothing is where there's no energy, it's the lack of energy.

Dear Valerio, I think the human mind deserves a prize for conceiving of the Infinite, an idea seeming to exist only there, in the mind. I must confess, after the initial letdown, I then felt proud to belong to the race of so-called *homo sapiens* who'd concocted something that doesn't exist in nature. To such a lofty and altogether superfluous meditation, artists too have contributed their fair share over the millennia. And so, before going, I'd like to leave you with the pages of a hypothetical story, completely incomplete, this humble *work in progress* expanding toward an infinite entirely our own, a poor, portable infinite, made just for those who insist on thinking that Nothing exists out there, while the Infinite continues to exist only deep down inside us.

For this limited-expansion story, the *genius loci* seems fitting, a good rule of thumb. Your paintings, too, seem fitting, especially their outlines done in sinopia, which as you know, can be filled with infinite colors. I've given my little story the working title, *The Minotaur's Headaches*. But I'll write it down for you tomorrow, before I go.

# Outside Terraces,
# Inside Terraces

The waiter arrived with a bottle of *Água das Pedras*, poured for us, asked if we wanted ice, and when we said no, gave a slight nod and disappeared. It didn't feel like winter, it felt more like spring. No, it *was* spring. The wisteria on the terrace was blooming, below was the grand stairway of Bom Jesus, with its Baroque chapels. Down from the hills, the city sparkled.

Listen, Davide, I said, we're in Braga, a name that comes from Bracara Augusta, an ancient Roman city – I think that's what it was in Latin– I don't know why we're here, why I brought you here, do you know? He sipped his water and smiled. Of course I do, he answered, because I had an appointment. Then he stood, turned away from me, and took in the view. Davide, I said, what appointment, who were you meeting? Just then my Portuguese translator Maria da Piedade Ferreira showed up, she'd been with us the night before and took good care of us. Maria da Piedade has read many books, and is now a publisher in Lisbon. Please, Maria da Piedade, I said, I've realized I don't know why we came to Braga after such a long journey, might you know the reason why?

I tried to think, I pressed my fists against my temples. Was there no reason? Not one reason why? I finished my *Água* and thought about what a Portuguese friend once told me, years ago, that *Água das Pedras* doesn't just cleanse the body; it cleanses the mind. But my mind wasn't cleansed. Something was weighing on me, something puzzling. So I stood up, and went and joined Davide on the stairway of Bom Jesus, where I told him: Davide, I don't know why we came, I don't know what appointment we had here. He smiled again and invited me to accompany him down the stairs. The hundreds of steps of the Bom Jesus stairway lead down to the city of Braga, now and then you reach a stone bench by a low wall where you can see the city and all the stairs you've just come down.

We stopped at the second bench. Looking up, Davide blinked and said: You see? Look. I looked. See that terrace? he asked. It was the wisteria terrace of our hotel, an old wooden terrace, with an ancient, winding wisteria vine. All right then, Davide said, I had an appointment with that terrace, I just didn't realize, and neither did you, but sometimes destiny leads us where we want even if we don't realize it. All right then, I was longing for that terrace, I didn't realize I was longing for that terrace – no – for every terrace in the world, and that terrace, seen from various angles, is already in my spirit, I'm not sure you understand what

I'm saying, I need oxygen and terraces where I can look at the world, I need to look at the world and I want to look at the world from terraces.

And where might these terraces be? I asked, knowing my question was obvious. He smiled again and answered: they're everywhere, but most of all, they're inside me, but in the meantime, we'll start with this. Under his arm was a sketchbook. He opened it and showed me a drawing.

And only then did I understand why we came to Braga.

# Parisian Cafés

"This is not Verlaine."

This book could begin with the same line Magritte wrote beneath his celebrated pipe (*Ceci n'est pas une pipe*), hinting that beneath this seemingly innocuous pipe there lay something more. Because reality isn't always as it seems. And in fact, this anonymous gentleman, so carefully rendered in Vincenzo Nisivoccia's pencil-drawing, is not Verlaine, and couldn't be. It's his "double," a customer in a Paris café who's borrowed Verlaine's likeness. Why? A mystery. Who knows: maybe the *République Française* – so proud of its literary achievements – has drummed up some scheme to tout its cultural heritage: might this be an actor sent around by the Tourist Board?

One thing is certain: Vincenzo Nisivoccia's book could only originate in Paris. And only in a café. This alternative sacred space, on the verge of extinction (or already extinct) in Italy, but bravely holding on in France, the foundation of a noble cultural tradition in Europe, the meeting place of conversation and communal life.

Paris, the cafés of Paris, the *terrasses* of the cafés of Paris. France has made a symbol of them, like the croissant and cup of coffee on a small round table, like oysters and *soupe à l'oignon*. Two particularly famous cafés are the *Flore* and *Les deux Magots*, their walls hung with photos of the writers and intellectuals who went there: Jean Paul Sartre, Simone de Beauvoir, Boris Vian, Louis Aragon and Elsa Triolet, the Surrealists, Picasso, Jacques Prévert. And even today, Parisian intellectuals will still converge there, frequently "in uniform": a rumpled jacket, a scarf (often red) tied around the neck, corduroy trousers: intellectuals I've heard Italians refer to as "the caviar left." But I don't think they eat much caviar; intellectuals, in France and everyplace else, just scrape by, especially in this world where books are read less and less; they'll just take a cup of coffee, like everyone else, also because a cup of coffee in these two cafés will cost as much as caviar, but it does give a person permission to sit at a table. And in these cafés, you can really be *alone* at a table.

But you don't have to go to the historical cafés to observe the colorful Parisian fauna, all the varied faces, with such interesting expressions, they're like a breath of fresh air, and they make you think the world's not made up of only the dull-witted – with eyes glazed over from watching television – like you'll find pretty much everywhere in Italy.

And it's from these varied faces – from a humanity that's still alive, non-homogenized, expressive, one that doesn't make you think humankind is climbing back down Darwin's evolutionary ladder – that Vincenzo Nisivoccia has created his figurative cast of characters. The stroke here is essential, very much restrained, at times only part of the face emerges, as if the rest doesn't matter – what's essential has been caught. And what's essential is the character. Looking at these faces is like reading La Bruyère's *Les Caractères*: the sad old man; the lady, faded but still hopeful; the poet; the thinker; the drifter; the idler; the handsome man; the part-time philosopher. But they're all so real, so vibrant, and looking at them is so heartening, because they make us feel that the world is still human, not made up of robots obeying the laws of the masses.

I ask myself if the author of these portraits, beyond being an artist, might also be considered an anthropologist or psychoanalyst. All three at once, I think, as artists are, who have the privilege of making us a mirror to give us back our own image.

REQUIEM

ANTONIO TABUCCHI

# For a Catalogue That Isn't

Bartolomeu Cid dos Santos used to etch imaginary maps into a plate, then smear sepia ink on top, producing prints like daguerreotypes from a timeless time and a placeless place; occasionally a shadow might slip over the maps, a figure in a hat who evoked Fernando Pessoa, or he'd create a labyrinth, or expansive arches down a hallway in perspective that took you where your imagination wanted to go; and there were also vaguely gothic castles, with a sphere that seemed to have rolled down from some other geometry, reminding you of Pascal's sphere because you understood its center was nowhere, yet there it was, its circumference everywhere.

And he made prints of flowers, or simulated flowers, a bit like Beardsley's, floral flowers, you might say. That after '74 – after the so-called Carnation Revolution and Portugal's return to democracy – were mainly carnations. As though the carnation was more than a flower, was an epoch-shaping corolla, a barrier against any return to fascism.

But I met Bartolomeu much earlier, before carnations came to mean what they did in his artwork and in the history of his country. That must have been in 1970, during a family gathering, because we had family in common. So our connection goes well beyond his artwork and my interest in his artwork. In that period he'd already been teaching Graphic Arts for many years at the Slade School of Fine Art in London; he'd go to Lisbon in the summer, but his house was in Sintra, the medieval hill town near Lisbon that Byron and Shelley both loved. And in that ancient house filled with books, objects, paintings, with wine cellars chilly enough for a sweater, we saw each other often, especially after the Carnation victory. Bartolomeu kept some prints he'd made in England over the winter in large portfolios held together with tape; these he stored in an enormous brass magazine rack shaped like a fan and once used as a fireplace screen, and he'd sort through these prints, to show his friends: you like this one of Don Quixote on bony old Rocinante? Take it, then. You like this Map of Desire? Take it, then.

Life is curious, made up of coincidences. One day, some copies of my *Requiem* in English translation arrived from London. In the package I found a letter from the publisher that basically said: "I hope you like the choice of cover art, since you left this up to us. It's a print by a Portuguese artist living in London who's well-known for his graphic art and pictures where imaginary maps often appear, evoking antique maps of Portugal, with the shade – the ghost, really – of a great poet who also appears in your novel."

A few days later, Bartolomeu called. "An English publisher asked if he could use one of my prints for some Italian novel set in Lisbon. I didn't know who the writer was – I only realized it was you when the book arrived."

Every August, Bartolomeu would celebrate his birthday in his old house in Sintra. The meal was at two in the afternoon, in an enormous room with a vaulted ceiling, like a terrace overlooking old Paço Real: around sixty people, more at times, friends of Bartolomeu, old-guard utopians, then the new-guard: the hard-core and the skeptical utopians on the left. We ate at wooden tables, on convent benches, the food tended toward Maghreb and South-Asian cuisine, couscous, curry, tajine, with salads from Sintra's vegetable gardens. The chef was Fernanda, Bertolomeu's companion, a simultaneous interpreter by profession, and an expert like few others on international cuisine and cinema.

For Christmas, Bartolomeu would send his friends a small lithograph. In recent times, he'd done fewer carnations, had replaced carnations with tanks and bombs, with small clownish figures shouldering submachine guns; on the horizon, you could just make out the lines of minarets, and the clowns vaguely resembled a president of the United States.

But the larger prints, the maps of desire, stubbornly resisted, and so did the sphere with its circumference everywhere and its center nowhere. The truth is, utopias are fragile, but if they become art they don't fear time. They earn an eternity all their own, and a beauty unafraid of styles blown in on the wind. Such is the work of Bartolomeu Cid dos Santos.

I would have liked to write this piece for one of Bartolomeu's catalogues. But, as we all know, sometimes, almost always, death is quicker than we are.

At times, I have referred to others' English translations of cited poems:

pp.55–56: Wislawa Szymborska, "Tortures," translated by Stanisław Barańczak and Clare Cavanagh.

p.59: Jorge Luis Borges, from "Ariosto and the Arabs," translated by Anthony Kerrigan.

pp.95–6: Carlos Drummond de Andrade, "In the Middle of the Road,"referring to translations by Elizabeth Bishop and Richard Zenith.

p.116: Wislawa Szymborska, from "Allegro Ma Non Troppo," translated by Stanisław Barańczak and Clare Cavanagh.

p.179: The epigraph is taken from Giacomo Leopardi's Fragment XXXVIII, in Jonathan Galassi's translation.

I wish to thank Jill Schoolman, Publisher of Archipelago Books, for all her support of literature in translation. My translation of this book was assisted greatly by the time and support of The National Endowment for the Arts and the University of Iowa's Translator-in-Residence Program. I also wish to thank Scott Kallstrom for his generous time and his patience, and my sister, the painter, Anne Harris, for her help with the art terminology. Finally, I am deeply grateful to Dr. Louise Rozier, for her encouragement over the years and for her many wonderful suggestions about this particular book.

—Elizabeth Harris

# *Art*

**Camilla Adami**

    p.158   *Primate*, 2001

**Valerio Adami**

    p.ii    *Portrait of Antonio Tabucchi*, 2000
    © 2020 Artists Rights Society (ARS), New York / ADAGP, Paris

    p.100  *Le minotaure*, 1996
    © 2020 Artists Rights Society (ARS), New York / ADAGP, Paris

    p.158  *A Love*, 1990
    © 2020 Artists Rights Society (ARS), New York / ADAGP, Paris

    p.178  *The Child's Time to Sleep (Holbein)*, 1993
    © 2020 Artists Rights Society (ARS), New York / ADAGP, Paris

**José Barrias**

    p.22    from the cycle, *Midday*, 1992
    from the book José Barrias, *Tempo*, 1992, Verona
    Love at first sight editions
    Photograph of the art by Veronica Simionato

p.22    *The Zuiderzee Dam Closure*
from the book José Barrias, *Tempo*, 1992, Verona
Love at first sight editions
Photograph of the art by Veronica Simionato

## Hippolyte Bayard

p.90    *Autoportrait en noyé*, c.1840

## Davide Benati

p.16    *Flames*, 1988
watercolor on paper on canvas
140 × 120 cm
Torino, Italy
courtesy of Mr. Piero Chiambretti

p.104   *Night Snow*, 2000
oil and serigraphe on canvas
180 × 180 cm
Bologna, Italy
Courtesy of GAM

p.190   *Terraces*, 1995
Oil on canvas
150 × 150 cm
courtesy of the artist

**Bartolomeu Cid dos Santos**

p.198   *Memória de Lisboa*, 1990

**António Costa Pinheiro**

p.154   *Fernando Pessoa Ele-Mesmo*, 1976
Oil on canvas
145 ×145 cm
courtesy of the artist's estate

**António Dacosta**

p.62   *A caça ao anjo*, 1984
Acrylic paint on canvas
134 × 168.5 cm
Col. Assembleia Legislativa da Região Autónoma dos Açores
Catalogue Raisonné inv. no. ADP173
Work photographed by Paulo Costa/FCG

**José de Guimarães**

p.126   *Femme-automobile*, 1987
Private Collection

**Münir Göle**

p.86   *Untitled*, 2007
Courtesty of the Artist

**Asian cap** from the collection of Ioanna Koutsoudaki  p.130

## Alberto Magnelli

p.94    *Untitled*, 1931
Blue ink on paper
26.8 × 20 cm
© 2020 Artists Rights Society (ARS), New York / ADAGP, Paris

## Giuseppe Modica

p.28    *Pessoa's Terrace*, 1993
Oil on panel
100 × 120 cm
Courtesy of the artist

## Oreste Fernando Nannetti

p.172    *Graffiti on the walls of the asylum of Volterra*, 1961–72

## Vincenzo Nisivoccia

p.194    *Nine o'clock at Café de Flore*, 2010

## Tullio Pericoli

p.6    *Postcard from Florence*, 1983
Watercolor and ink on paper
p.162    *Robert Louis Stevenson*, 1986
Watercolor and ink on paper
56 × 38 cm

## Piero Pizzi Cannella

p.34   *Faraway*, 2001–2002
Mixed media on canvas
220 × 150 cm
© Archivo Pizzi Cannella

p.166   *Untitled*, 1998-1999
Oil on canvas
270 × 150 cm
© Archivo Pizzi Cannella

## Júlio Pomar

p.138   *The Barrister* (or *Advogado*), 1999
Crayons and oil pastel on paper
© Júlio Pomar

## Paula Rego

p.80   *Untitled*, 2003
This *azulejo*|tile is exclusively produced by Ratton Cerâmicas
from an original work by Paula Rego
*Fire*, limited edition
©Ratton Cerâmicas

## Lisa Santos Silva

p.72   *La religieuse portugaise*, 1999
Oil on canvas
130 × 97 cm
Courtesy of the artist

## Giancarlo Savino

p.40 *Into the Dark of the Night* (detail), 1993
Watercolor
30 × 24 cm

## Antonio Seguí

p.52 *Ça bouge*, 1980
Pastel on paper
80 × 60 cm
© 2020 Artists Rights Society (ARS)
New York / ADAGP, Paris

## Alessandro Tofanelli

p.46 *Sooner or Later*, 2008
Oil on wood
50 × 50cm

## Maria Helena Vieira da Silva

p.110 *La partie d'échecs* (detail), 1943
© 2020 Artists Rights Society (ARS), New York / ADAGP, Paris

## Giancarlo Vitali

p.150 *Portrait of Pereira*, 1996
Acquaforte and acquatinte
© ArchiviVitali

*archipelago books*
is a not-for-profit literary press devoted to
promoting cross-cultural exchange through innovative
classic and contemporary international literature
www.archipelagobooks.org